The Supornatural Collection
Volume One

Edited by Gio Lassater

Inkubus Publishing

ISBN-10:0692666206
ISBN-13:978-0692666203

Raising the Stakes first appeared in *Blood in the Rain*,
published by Cwtch Press

Contents

Unleashed

By Gio Lassater

I was 18 when I lost my virginity. A late start, I know. But it was worth it. His name was Lyle. I still remember how it all began. The way he looked at me. Touched my leg playfully but with meaning. The orange light of the cassette player in his tan Chevette cast a glare across his glasses, obscuring his eyes.

While Wilson Phillips told us to hold on, Lyle pulled off Highway 15 into the driveway of an abandoned house. The family who owned it used it for rent when they moved to a much nicer house a few miles away. As far as we knew, the last people to live there had moved out six months before. Ghostly curtains partially obscured a few windows. Full moonlight lit the wood-fenced yard.

Lyle spread a blanket over the cracked concrete slab outside the back door. A car sped past on the highway, causing both of us to stop in sudden fear of being discovered. It moved on; we breathed.

I don't remember exactly how the conversation had started. Did I outright say I was gay? Did Lyle? Did it matter? I guess not, but it's amazing the things you think about when you're wondering how it will feel to have a dick in your mouth for the first time.

We had made a pact to tell each other if we found the other one attractive. I think things had been building to this point for some time. Lyle's girlfriend had been my friend for a few years. When they started dating, Lyle and I began hanging out. Driving the back roads of my hometown. And let's face it, all the roads in that hell hole were back roads.

Eventually, the three of us hanging out led to us dropping her off at curfew and going back out. The cemetery. Dragging Main. Finding the quickest way between towns in the dark while wind whipped through the windows and our hair.

God, were we lame.

But, being lame isn't so bad when you have company. And hearing someone else echo thoughts you've never told anyone else about is the most liberating experience you can ever imagine. So innocent. Pure. Liberating.

Frightening as hell.

I sat on the blanket, staring up at Lyle towering over me. That was the only way he could be taller than I was. Five-five isn't much compared to six-one. But he was suddenly immense, standing over me. Unzipping his pants.

My heart beat faster. This was it. The moment of truth. No turning back. Another car sped along the highway, but I couldn't be bothered. I had seen the Promised Land, and it was amazing.

I stared at the first real dick that wasn't attached to my body. I touched it. Surely God stood poised to strike us both dead. Inflict a dread scourge upon us. I grasped it.

Thick.

Hot.

God, help me. I'm sure he enjoyed that prayer.

"Do you want to stop?" The words were a hiss from Lyle's lips.

I looked up. Saw the black holes where his eyes should be. He licked his lips. My mind screamed *No*. I asked, "Do you want me to stop?"

Suddenly he became speechless. Shook his head. Thrust his dick through my fingers. Closer to my lips. My tongue darted out. Tasted salt.

God, help me.

I'm a fag. No denying it now. Dad will be happy to know he was right about me. Dad likes to be right.

Dick tastes good.

Lyle cursed as I slid him into my mouth. He was no virgin, and I took it as a compliment that I had him quivering. Standing on his toes. Running fingers through my hair.

I pulled more of him into my mouth. Hairs tickled my nose, making me laugh. That is a hard thing to do with a dick in your mouth, in case you were wondering. I spat him out, choking on spit and laughter.

"It's not you," I promised. Pain was on his face. I replaced it with pleasure. So much pleasure.

I lost track of time.

"Can I fuck you?"

The words hung on the moonbeams washing over us. I nodded, removing my pants. He positioned me how he wanted me. Kicked his clothes onto the dirty concrete. I watched him over my shoulder. He lined up. Pushed forward.

This is usually the part of the story where the camera either cuts to the two people waking up the next morning, or you get to see something that sends you for a box of Kleenex. Usually.

This is actually the part of the story where we pause for a public service announcement. It's not about AIDS, condoms, pre-marital sex, or anything like that. No, this is where virgins are given the best piece of advice they can possibly ever hear.

Lube is your friend.

Don't believe me? Let a guy push his dick into your ass without it. Go on. I'll wait. Once you finish screaming, come back and tell me how right I was. I promise not to look you in the eye.

Yeah.

Shoving a dry tree trunk inside a doughnut is not something you do without plenty of slick, slippery help.

Tears stung my eyes. I screamed and scooted forward. I would never be able to sit down again. I just knew it.

"I'm so sorry," Lyle said, falling to his knees. "I'm so very sorry. I didn't think about it."

Yeah, tell that to my ass, damn you.

So, remember when I told you I lost my virginity. This wouldn't technically be that time. At least, not as far as I'm concerned.

The night I truly lost my virginity, it was in the back of Lyle's Chevette. And there was lots of lube. I straddled him. Rode him. Pushed the suspension of that shitty car to the limits. God, it was amazing.

What I didn't count on was how it would make me feel afterward. I'm not talking about the euphoria or the regret of "What have I done?" I'm talking about, "Holy shit! I'm no longer a virgin. How can I go home? Mom and Dad are going to realize I'm not a virgin anymore." Like there is some gigantic neon sign that appeared over my head that screamed in vibrant red, "I took it up the ass and loved it."

But that was exactly what I feared. I walked through the off-white front door. There they sat on the reclining love seat. Watching the TV that sat on top of the TV that hadn't worked in five years. Jeff Foxworthy studied my family for his eventual routines.

They ignored me. But, I'm not a virgin anymore! You didn't notice! Where's the disappointment? The accusations? The tears? Well, shit, this is a relief. And a letdown, oddly enough.

I mumbled good night and went to bed. Lying in the darkness and post-virginity bliss. And confusion.

The next morning on the way to school I sat in the spot in the seat that took me farther than I thought I'd ever want to go. I probably should have felt guilty about being 'the other woman,' but I didn't.

After that, shit got weird.

It started with *Cat People*. That's a movie, in case you were wondering. Don't waste your time. It's a piece of shit. I only mention it because it was the impetus for what became the bat-shit-craziest three months of my life.

I don't know what went on in Lyle's brain, but something seriously skewed. It started with that movie. And then there were others. Werewolves. Vampires. More cat people. Lyle became convinced it was all real. Convinced he was a shape shifter of some sort.

That culminated in us standing in front of a rock-facade church in the middle of fucking nowhere. Small towns. They're bat-shit-crazy, too. Who puts a church at the end of a gravel road that adjoins a cattle guard leading to government pasture land?

But there it was. And Lyle was showing me the skull in the wall. Now, let me clarify for you that it wasn't an actual skull. Lyle just thought the rocks on the front wall of the church lined up in the perfect representation of a skull. If I squinted enough and let my brain fall out of my head, I could see it.

These people were obviously not Christians. They were Satan worshippers in disguise. Just ask Lyle. He'd tell you.

And then there was the coven of witches that stalked the State park north of the town. We never found them. To my eternal gratitude, let me tell you.

Do you remember earlier when I mentioned eighteen and stupid? Yeah, that didn't change. Lyle soon convinced me this was all real. I was a werewolf. We were a pack. I was probably willing to believe anything to get him to keep fucking me.

Before long, the alcohol drowned out the real world. Helped us stay in the supernatural world of lycanthropes, satanic churches, and the ghosts of Indian princesses haunting the mesas they had been flung from. We actually saw her one night. Seriously.

Well, maybe not. But, whatever.

Life became two different roads traveled. Sometimes simultaneously. Sometimes separately. At school, everything was normal. At night, we watched each other with baited breath, wondering who would fully transform first.

Lyle claimed his incisors could elongate, grow, sharpen. Whether through shadows or a genuine desire to believe, we saw it. I became so wrapped up in the mysteries we were trying to unravel that I started seeing things. Black shapes and blurs that darted from one side of doors to another. They stalked from closets at night. Peeked over the sill of the window overlooking my bed. Sometimes they moved too quickly to be sure they were real. Other times, I wished I could stop seeing them.

Alcohol became my second lover. Helped me to escape. Forced me to see them more. Face what they really were. Demons were upset we had tread into their domain. They had come to claim us. We had fucked up.

Still, we didn't stop. We pushed farther. Truly sought transformation.

Through blood.

Sex.

That was where Darren came in. He was my uncle's best friend from high school. He was a functional alcoholic and sometimes petty criminal, and, damn, he was hot as hell. Long brown hair. Deep brown eyes. A chiseled, hirsute chest that lead into abs even Michelangelo would have had difficulty sculpting. His legs, so sturdy. An ass you could eat cake from. My God! He was a wet dream come to life.

Lyle wanted him. I wanted him. We could use his energy to push our transformations past the point we'd reached so far. Not just incisors but full metamorphosis. The wolf released.

We talked Darren into going camping with us. It was a long discussion over several weeks. He was working a lot, with very little time off, but he assured us as soon as he could, he would join us.

We planned. Prepared. Stocked up on plenty of alcohol. It would help us get Darren where we needed him. Vulnerable. Malleable.

The wait was torture.

But finally the day arrived. We found Darren at a party his friends were having on a typical Friday night. Even though he hadn't been drinking, he was definitely relaxed. No shirt. No shoes. I wanted to service him.

We talked for a while. Well, shouted really. Shitty music at full blast. You know, the kind that begs someone to get pissed off and call the cops. Darren asked us to hang out for a while. We had the whole weekend. No rush.

Four hours later, Lyle and I were so horny we could barely stand. Just watching Darren was enough to keep me nearly hard the entire night. I fanaticized about blowing him right there. In front of everyone.

Of course, the follow up in that dream was getting the shit beat out of me by all the rednecks at the party. That would be the definition of anti-climactic.

Finally, Darren was ready. One o'clock in the morning. I had passed out on the couch. Luckily no one had drawn a dick on my face. Darren pulled me from the couch. Steadied me as I stared around groggily. A mixture of booze and sleep had me wondering where I was.

The feel of Darren's bare flesh on my arm helped wake me up. I saw his chest. Felt the hair brush along my skin. Better than coffee.

Darren sat in the back seat on the ride to the lake. He'd been drinking heavily and passed out before we pulled onto the main street of town. His snores were loud. Filled the car. Rivaled the New Kids on the Block hanging tough in the speakers.

"I can't wait to see him naked," Lyle said. He watched Darren in the rearview mirror. I heard Lyle's pants unzip. "Damn, my dick has been crushed so much tonight. Here, hold the wheel."

I steered with my left hand from the passenger side, watching Lyle scoot upward in his seat. His pants were soon at his knees. His dick plopped against the steering wheel. He tugged it a couple times before resuming driving.

"Suck it for me?" he requested.

I never had to be asked twice to suck dick. I lived for it. Leaning across the center console, burying the emergency brake handle into my chest, I pulled Lyle into my mouth. He hissed and jerked the car back onto the road.

"Shit. I never get tired of that." He patted the back of my head as I slid up and down his shaft. Pressed it into my throat.

Lyle moaned. Darren echoed him from the back seat.

I sat up suddenly. My eyes glued on Darren. My breath ragged in my chest from the adrenaline instantly racing through my veins. He was still asleep.

I resumed my task.

Lyle's dad was a State Game Warden. The lake we were going to was part of his jurisdiction. Lyle spent a lot of time with his dad, and because of that, he knew where all the secluded and hidden spots were on the lake. As tree limbs and river grass scraped along the sides of the Chevette, he inched us into one of the more remote spots of the lake. Only the game wardens could access it.

Well, them and their kid who borrowed the keys to the lock.

I pulled the gate closed behind us, reset the lock, and jumped into the car.

Darren awoke when the door slammed shut. He yawned and stretched. "We almost there?" he asked.

"Yes," Lyle said.

"Good. I've got to piss bad." Darren squeezed his crotch and repositioned himself in the seat.

Lyle stopped several feet from the water's edge. The headlights washed over the tent we had set up earlier in the afternoon. Darren stumbled into the trees to empty his bladder. Lyle and I lit the fire. Sat beside it. Whispered our plan.

Darren trudged back to us. Warmed his hands over the fire. Stared up at the full moon. "It's beautiful here. Well, for night time."

"It's pretty nice during the day, too," Lyle promised. "And the fishing is good. If you want to do any."

Darren nodded. I handed him a beer. He popped the top and took a long drink. Sighed in appreciation.

"So," Darren said, "did you guys bring me out here to fuck me?"

I almost shit my pants. Lyle laughed nervously when Darren stared at us and laughed loudly. It echoed across the water. A bird in the distance screeched. Darren drunkenly mimicked it, laughing more.

"Do you want us to fuck you?" Lyle asked.

I couldn't believe what I was hearing. This was not how we had planned this. Where was the seduction? The subtlety? For God's sake, he is going to beat the shit out of us and throw our faggot bodies into the lake!

I bit my lip.

Darren looked at me. Looked at Lyle.

"You two little shits have been staring at me for weeks." Darren took a long drink of beer. Emptied it. Crushed the can and tossed it into the darkness. "You're eyes have fucked me so many times. You beat your dicks thinking about me?" he asked.

I looked away. Embarrassed. Man, did I! I had spewed so much come thinking about Darren it wasn't even funny. I'm surprised I didn't run dry.

Lyle didn't move. He was a rock. Implacable. "Does that turn you on, Darren? Apparently you don't have a problem with it since you agreed to come with us."

I hadn't thought of that.

Darren smiled. "You two little fags think you're so smart, huh?" He grabbed another beer and downed half of it. "Come here." He pointed at me. Beckoned with his finger.

I looked at Lyle. He nodded. Slowly I walked to Darren, attempting to hide the hard protrusion in my blue jeans. Standing in front of my desire, I looked into his eyes. At his chest. His crotch. Back at his eyes.

He reached out. Ran the palm of his hand over my denim-caged dick. "You're going to hurt yourself. Pull that thing out so I can see it."

My fingers fumbled with the button and zipper. I stared at Darren staring at my groin. Watching me as I revealed myself to him.

"Nice," he said. Licked his lips.

9

Pants fell to my knees. Darren snaked his fingers inside my underwear. Ran along my dick. Electricity fried me.

"Don't come. Not from just a touch," Darren admonished.

"I won't," I promised.

For several minutes Darren played with me. When he finally pulled my underwear down, I gasped. He stared at my dick. Wiped the pre-come from the head. Licked his fingers clean.

"Turn around. Bend over."

I followed his orders. Stared into the fire. Its warmth bathed my face while the heat from Darren's hand warmed my ass. Lyle watched us. Pulled his dick out through his open fly. Stroked his rigid dick with a blissful smile. He nodded at me. Licked his lips.

Darren ran a hand over my smooth ass. Kissed it. Caressed it. I felt his calloused fingers kneading the white flesh. I moaned. He moaned.

His finger brushed along my crack. Pushed in. Gently. Slowly. Lovingly.

I grunted when he circled my hole.

"You have a nice ass," Darren told me.

"Wait till you fuck it," Lyle offered. "He's so tight. So deep. Better than any pussy you've ever had. He'll ruin you for women. Promise."

I smiled. Lyle winked at me. I pushed back against Darren's finger. Moaned softly.

"Stand up."

Again I did as Darren ordered. He turned me around, wiped another drop from my dick, and studied it. It disappeared into his mouth, and he asked, "Do you like to suck cock?"

I nodded.

"You any good?"

"Damn right," I said proudly.

Darren smiled. "Good. Been too long since I had a decent blow job."

"You won't be disappointed." I looked down at his crotch. "Want me to show you?"

"Soon. Sit down." He looked at Lyle. "Your turn. Come here."

Lyle stood up slowly. His dick stuck out in front of him, swaying side to side as he sauntered over to Darren. Stood over him. His cock only inches from Darren's wet lips. "I don't suck cock," Lyle stated. "I don't get fucked."

Darren grabbed onto Lyle's dick. If Lyle's yelp was any indication, it hurt. "You listen to me, you little shit," Darren hissed. "I'm in charge here. Just because you're 18 doesn't make you anything other than an arrogant prick. I'm the man. I'm in charge. Your little plan you had? Yeah, you can just forget about that. If I want your ass wrapped around my cock, that's exactly what I'm going to get. Understood?"

"What if I tell everyone you raped me?" I could hear victory in Lyle's voice.

Darren laughed. "You know that party where everyone saw me tonight? I've fucked every woman there at least twice. All those guys are my friends. We've been through some shit together. Ain't none of them going to believe I'm a fag let alone tell a cop or judge anything at all. They'll say I was there all night. They'll say the only time they saw you two was when you got pissed off we wouldn't give or buy you beer. See how this works?"

Lyle nodded. Realization set in, by the look on his face.

"You're ass been fucked?" Darren wanted to know.

Lyle shook his head.

"Good." Darren finally released Lyle's dick. The smirk on his face was just this side of evil.

Lyle turned around to walk back to me.

Darren smacked his ass hard through the blue denim. Killed the last of his beer. He leaned back into the grass, resting on his elbows. He stared up at the stars. The Milky Way spread across the sky, bearing witness.

A deep, guttural growl rumbled in Darren's chest.

I closed my eyes. Let the sound wash over me. Crickets fell silent. A frog or fish splashed in the lake a few feet away. Something within

11

me stirred. Drawn to Darren, I walked slowly, nakedly to him. Stood over him, eyes closed, soul open. The growl continued.

I fell to my knees and buried my face in his crotch. The rough material of his pants rubbed against my cheeks. I could smell oil and chemicals. Sweat. I felt pre-come dripping from my cock. I swiped it with a finger. Held it out to Darren.

He licked it clean while unbuttoning his pants. I pulled them down. Within minutes his blue briefs were wet with spit and pre-come. I swiped at the head of his dick which slid above the waistband along his obliques. The growling had stopped, but when Darren grasped the back of my head, I felt the same electric fire racing through me.

I ripped his underwear from him, not realizing what I was doing. As soon as his dick sprang upward, I opened my mouth, and Darren shoved my head down. His cock hit the back of my throat. I gagged and tried to pull back, but Darren forced me down. I felt the shaft slide into my throat. Tears stung my eyes. I couldn't breathe. This never happened with Lyle.

Darren held me there with both hands. When I thought I was going to suffocate on cock, he slowly released me. Pulled back centimeters at a time. My lungs burned. Suddenly, air. I could breathe.

I choked and gasped. Darren slapped my cheeks with his spit-soaked cock. I looked up at him. Shivered when the moonlight glinted from his eyes.

"Do you still want me?"

"Yes," I gasped, nodding my head.

"Good." He waved his dick at me. "Show me what you've got."

In response, I buried his cock into my throat again. Reveled in his hissed curses. I rested my chin on his balls. Buried my nose in his thick thatch of pubic hair. The smell of him reminded me of locker rooms, sweaty men doing hard labor, and primal sex. I lost myself in his dick. His growls and moans and encouragement.

He leaned forward and found my ass again. Pulled my cheeks apart. Rubbed against my tight ring. His fingers circled. Tickled. Battered sweetly at my defenses. I willed myself to relax. Opened myself to him. The tip of his callused finger barely entered me. He held it there. Unmoving. Content to remain on the threshold of the most intimate part of me I was willing to give to him. If only he would take it.

I pushed back, hoping to force his finger into me. He pulled back. Kept his finger where it had been. I pushed back again. He slapped my ass with a hard, resounding smack that echoed into the trees and across the water.

"Stop."

The command struck me as hard as his hand had. I felt it in my soul and had no choice but to obey. I held my position on my knees and contented myself with nursing on his dick.

"Good boy." He held me down all the way on his cock again. This time I was ready. Instead of choking and gagging I constantly swallowed, working him with my throat. The growl returned.

When he released me, he pulled me up, disgorging his dripping cock from my mouth. Dragged on top of him, Darren kissed me deeply. Bruised my lips with his. I tasted alcohol and desire. I wormed my way up until I was straddling him. Ran my ass over his sloppy dick while mine bounced over the washboard of his abs.

"You want me to fuck you?"

"Yes," I said, looking deeply into his eyes.

"I'm not sure you're ready." The way he said it filled me dread and a sudden need to have him inside me.

"Please." Even I could hear the begging tone in my voice. I felt ashamed and enflamed at the same time. He had awakened something in me I had never experienced with Lyle. Something I needed to prolong and nurture. "Fuck me."

He smiled. "There is no turning back."

I had no idea why he said that. I didn't want to turn back. It was destiny that he fuck me. Here. Now. Tonight beneath the light of the full moon. Wasn't this what Lyle and I had planned? To awaken the beast within? Complete the lupine transformation using Darren's sexual energy?

In response, I reached back, grasped his cock firmly in my fist and planted the head against my hole. "Fuck me."

He nodded once and slammed his cock into me without warning. I threw my head back and gasped loudly. Impaled myself until I felt his balls hit my ass. I sat on him, quivering. My legs felt like jelly. My ass burned and tingled.

I looked down and realized I had covered Darren's stomach, chest, and face with my come. But I was still rock hard.

Darren licked his lips. Cleaned his face with his hand and then bathed it with his tongue. I kissed him before he could swallow everything. Tasted myself on his lips. His tongue.

He pushed me up, pulling his cock out until only the head stayed inside me and then slammed me down again. Another small jet of come sprayed his abs. Before I knew it, Darren was standing up, clutching me in his arms. I wrapped my legs around his waist. Smashed our bodies together. Felt the sticky heat of my come gluing us into one sexual beast. I bounced up and down. Tested the limits of Darren's strength which seemed boundless.

He carried me toward the car. As we passed Lyle I saw him naked on the ground, furiously stroking his cock. Sweat slicked his body. His hair hung in wet strands. He ran a hand up Darren's leg. As soon as their flesh touched, Lyle screamed and came. He had never come so much. It bathed him the way I had covered Darren.

Lyle collapsed, completely spent. His chest heaved. His cock remained hard, as if he hadn't even touched it.

Darren slammed me onto the hood of the Chevette. The metal buckled and screeched beneath me. Distantly I knew it should have hurt, but the euphoria induced by Darren immediately jackhammering into me sent those thoughts flying to the farthest recesses of my mind.

Darren alternated his rhythm between fast and furious fucking and long, slow thrusts that buried him in me. Filled me. He bit into my shoulder. I clawed at his back. A breeze picked up and blew gently over us, carrying the scent of sex and come into the darkness.

Lyle was standing beside the car. His cock in his hand. He and Darren kissed furiously. I leaned over, pushed Lyle's hand away, and pulled his dick into my mouth. He fucked my mouth with the same intensity and lack of mercy Darren showed my ass. I opened up and let him use me.

I have no idea how long we were locked together before Lyle threw his head back and roared. Taking my cue, I clamped my lips tightly on his cock and swallowed as much of the deluge as I could. No matter how quickly I drank it down, it seemed like there was no end to the come geyser. It dribbled from my lips. Finally, I spit Lyle's dick out and let him coat my chest.

Inexplicably I felt a burning heat begin to suffuse my body. Darren stared down at me. He pushed himself all the way into my ass and growled, "Here it comes."

Darren exploded inside me. I started milking him for everything he had. But within seconds the heat inside me became too much to bear. I screamed. I heard popping. Felt pain and fire coursing through my veins. Darren picked me up. Smashed our bodies together.

"Change," he growled into my ear.

"What?" My brain was hazy. Sweat dripped from every pore. Come dripped from my abused ass.

The world suddenly exploded. I threw my head back and screamed. Darren's teeth clamped onto my neck. I felt liquid warmth run down my chest. When he pulled away, his face was a mass of black fur and red-tinged teeth.

"Change," he commanded in a guttural mixture of sex god and demonic hound.

He flipped me over. Continued fucking me. His fingernails-now-claws left long jagged gouges in the dented metal hood. Looking at them, I realized the black furry paws belonging to Darren were beside

15

my own shaggy brown paws. I ran a suddenly long, thick tongue over my sharp teeth. Tasted and smelled the remnants of Lyle's come.

Lyle.

I turned. Stared at him.

Still human.

I could smell his fear. His sweat and come. His desire.

"Change me," he begged. I could see the longing in his eyes.

Shaking Darren off me, I tried to say something to Lyle, but the words were a growl and bark. Lyle backed away from the car. His hands held in front of him.

I leapt from the car. My paws slammed into Lyle's chest. Drove him to the ground. My saliva dripped onto his face.

Darren moved quickly behind me. He sank his cock back into my ass as my teeth sank into the tender, sweet flesh of Lyle's throat.

In the distance, a night bird screamed.

This Old, Lonely Road

By Francis Maddox

The rain had stopped, but droplets still sluiced down the car's back window. The moisture on the windshield had finally cleared. Lucky, because I may not have seen him otherwise. Tall, thin, and all covered up in an evergreen rain poncho, the hitchhiker was waving me down. He held up a soaked cardboard sign that read, "SEATTLE." There was no question that I would be picking him up. After all, my cap was brown and quickly drying. Every second, and my hunger grew more desperate.

I turned my cap back with my free hand so that the bill didn't obscure my vision. As I slowed down, the guy in the poncho folded up the sign, picked up a small duffel bag, and ran towards my hatchback.

I stopped and pushed the button that rolled down the passenger window. The man slowed to a trot and placed both of his wet hands over my passenger door.

"How far are you going?" he asked eagerly.

I smiled. "All the way to Seattle." I wasn't, but his eyes were a deep, entrancing brown, and his skin seemed especially soft. How I love the feel of soft skin parting against my teeth! I pushed the shifter into park, all four doors unlocking in response. He took that as a cue to open the passenger door.

His choice. I grinned widely.

He planted himself down on my passenger seat, pulling off the poncho. He was wearing a hoodie underneath and jeans that were torn at the knees and at the thighs. His black hair was unkempt and hadn't been cut in a while. He shivered and threw the poncho and his bag into my backseat. He didn't appear to notice my iron pike, lying on the floor in the back, the blood coating the sharp end long-dry.

When he closed the door, I shifted the car into drive and merged back onto the road.

"Thanks for picking me up," he said. "I'm Cal."

"And cold." There is power in a name, and I knew instantly that Cal wasn't his. "Want me to turn on the heater?"

"Oh god, yes!" He smiled at me.

I looked at the dashboard for the first time, trying to figure out the controls. There were many, brightly lit and wearyingly confusing. I managed to turn the fan on, but the air the vents expelled was frigid.

"I'm sorry," I said. "This is a newish car."

"Do you mind?" he asked, his hand rising to meet the panel beneath the radio.

"Be my guest."

He turned the heater on to maximum, and then he did the same to the fan.

"Weren't you cold?" he asked.

I shook my head. "I'm very hairy," I said proudly. I was watching him more closely than most people would, and he seemed to notice because he started to look at me the same way.

"You're a bear, aren't you?"

I laughed. "I am very much like a bear, yes."

He unzipped the front of his hoodie slowly enough to draw my attention. He wasn't wearing a shirt underneath. His chest was smooth and hairless. I imagined him hanging nude, a hook pushed through gashes in his ankles between the tendon and the bone. There wouldn't be time for any of my brand of fun tonight, but I was looking forward to finding good places to eat in the city.

"I'm really grateful that you picked me up," he said, turning to face me so that one side of his open hoodie hung loosely from his shoulder, revealing his left breast. Although he was thin, his chest was so tight and sinewy. My mouth began to water. I licked my lips.

Turning my gaze back towards the still-slick road, I said, "How grateful are you?"

His hand landed on my thigh. His fingertips were on my groin.

"*Very* grateful."

I looked back at him, his eyes directed at the space between my legs. My lad stood at attention, as if it knew that it was being examined. It pressed against my pants and felt indecently pleasant.

"What would you do to repay me?" I asked him. In other times, a bowl of milk might suffice. He seemed to be offering something altogether different, and I was eager to see what that was.

"Do you want to pull over?" he asked. "Just keep the heater on."

"I do." I pulled over to the curb and set the car into park.

The hitchhiker's hand crawled onto the growing bulge in my pants and gripped it. "You're really big."

"I am," I said. I watched him as he unbuttoned my pants and unzipped them.

"I wanna suck you off," he said.

"Will it feel good?" I asked.

His hands slipped my dick out. It was veiny and hairy at its base. And it was rigid from his cold touch. "I like that you go commando."

I couldn't be sure what that meant—wearing no underwear, I supposed—but I grunted with approval and reached for his hair. I gripped it tightly in my hands, feeling the wet strands strain between my fingers.

He leaned in closer and wrapped his lips around my dick. He licked the head and then pushed it deep into his mouth. He swallowed, and I felt his palate press against me and release. I released a willful moan. "That *does* feel good."

What's-his-name made a muffled sound, but I wanted nothing more than for him to continue. I tightened my grip around his hair and pushed him deeper. I felt him gag, the muscles in the back of his throat tightening and relaxing against the head of my cock again and again. I felt a rush of blood flowing out of my head and into my groin as it throbbed against his tongue.

I wanted to call him by name—this felt like a situation that merited it—but he hadn't given me a real one. I wasn't going to call him by a falsehood. I groaned delightfully instead.

When I felt a rush of energy pouring into my crotch and fluids pushing out from me with the pressure of a heartbeat, he pulled his head away from me and grinned. His lips glistened and his eyes seemed to glow. This was a sort of magic, I was sure.

"I want to see your hairy bear chest," he said.

My instincts took over, and I tore my plaid shirt off. The buttons bounced onto the dashboard, our seats, and the floor. My chest was covered in curled fur that formed spirals around my hard nipples. He reached for my arms and pulled long sleeves back. He held my right forearm in his hands and pushed his long fingers along the thick hairs coating it.

"I love your bear arms," he said, hungrily. It was a familiar tone.

"I love your lips," I said.

"Do you want to kiss them?"

"I don't know how." I was being honest. I had never kissed another person. If my lips met another set, it was to grip them tight and feel them rend. I never considered the inimitable gaiety of a simple touch.

He put one of his hands over the back of my neck and pulled me towards him. Our lips pressed against each other, and his tongue pushed its way into my mouth. I licked the inside of his in return.

His hand rose over my head and touched the bill of my hat. I put my hand on his. "Don't," I said.

He pulled his tongue back and locked into my eyes. "You really like your dopey cap, huh?"

I nodded and wrapped my fingers in his. "It's important to me."

He tilted his head past my line of sight and bit my ear lobe, whispering, "I want you to fuck me."

"That sounds interesting," I said.

He reached for his hips and slipped off his jeans without unbuttoning them. He had also gone commando. His dick flicked upwards, slapping his belly, when it had been released from its denim bond. When he started to remove his hoodie, I reached forward and pulled his arms back, considering whether I wanted to keep him trapped by the sleeves.

He bit his bottom lip. "You're so strong."

"I am," I said. Then I settled on letting him free. The flesh I wore carried an insatiable instinct with it—something other than hunger—and it wanted to fuck him as badly as he wanted me to fuck him. "Prepare yourself," I said, hoping that he'd give me a new cue as to what to do.

He lifted himself on the seat and faced the window, lifting his ass towards me. Then he turned his head to face me with a welcoming countenance.

I raised myself up on my own seat, knowing my place instinctively. I gripped his bony hips and spat between his cheeks. My fingers spread the fluid further into his crack and slipped into his hole. I fingered him while he moaned, growing more exhilarated by the pleasure his sounds implied. I let my hands explore his belly and reach his nipples. Then I held tightly to him as my head pressed against his hole. I pushed my cock inside him with ease.

He whined pitifully, excitedly, ravenously.

I pulled my hips back and forth again, feeling the intensity of the electricity flickering from my pounding dick through my torso and into my ecstasy-addled brain. I thrust deeper, harder, finding myself groaning with greater intensity, until I felt an implacable flow of juices burst from my body into his.

He moaned wildly and held his own cock tightly, pulling to and fro, until translucent, white seed burst out of him and onto the seat he'd been straddling.

I fell back, feeling both weak and delighted in a way that only feeding had ever made me feel before. I looked into the rearview mirror, but my cap was still brown and growing every drier. But I felt myself, for the first time, not wanting to eat my passenger.

Then he turned around, his eyes were sunken in, and his flesh was ashen gray. His flat teeth had grown as sharp as mine could be.

"That was fun," he said, "but now I'm hungry."

He lunged at me and dug his sharp claws into my shoulders. I pushed against him and reached for my door, barely opening it in time to push myself out into the cold street. An oncoming car swerved out of the way to avoid hitting me, lost control on the wet road, and was violently stopped by a tree. The car I had been driving veered off the embankment, hurled grass and mud into the air, and stopped with a thud against the soft earth.

I ran and ripped open the back driver's side door, flakes of paint and metal spraying onto the ground. The hitchhiker made it out from the passenger's side and around the front of the car as I pulled my pike from its hiding place, now beneath his duffel bag. I held it out, sharp end pointed at the hitchhiker's neck. He watched me, his dick now flaccid and gray. But I couldn't stick him. He no longer smelled like food. He smelled like…me.

Moreover, I smelled blood—food—from the car that had nearly hit me. The one that had ground itself against the bark of a young sequoia.

The hitchhiker also seemed to smell it because he turned towards the car that had been crushed upon impact with the tree.

"I had fun," I said. "You had fun. And I think that now, we both need to eat. And my cap needs wet, *human* blood. Not whatever yours is."

The hitchhiker grimaced, displaying a deeply jagged row of teeth. I allowed my own teeth to grow sharp, too. To show him that neither of us were human, though he was obviously more experienced with a flesh body than I was.

"Wendigo," he said, as his bones cracked back into place and his skin turned from ash gray to its previous dark brown hue. "You looked so delicious."

"Red cap." I licked my lips. "So did you. But I think I'd like to do what we just did again." I motioned at the crashed stranger with my pike. "After. Wanna share?" I asked. "Then, we can fuck again."

"I like that idea," he said, a long finger slowly circling his left nipple. "Seattle is gonna to be so much fun."

I lowered the pike to my side and joined him in walking towards our new prey.

"I have to admit that I forgot the fake name you gave me," I said.

"I never cared for yours," he answered. "But we can trade names after we eat."

As we tore into the other vehicle and its lonely driver, my cap dripping with crimson life anew, I thought that today had been a good day.

Ménage à Troy

By Gio Lassater

Ares stood in the midst of bodies littering the killing field and gazed up at the massive stone walls of Troy. Scavenger birds circled lazily overhead, no doubt filled from gorging on the fallen soldiers. Silence surrounded him and stretched into the distance. He smiled at the handiwork of both the Trojans and the Greeks. If anyone knew how to pay homage to the god of war, those two civilizations did.

He turned his head to the side, and the breeze blew his long, curly black hair from his eyes. Pulling his blood-red cloak closer around his shoulders, he made his way through the detritus of the battleground. Zeus's words echoed in his ears, briefly tarnishing the enjoyment of the carnage around him. *End this damned war, Ares. End it, or I will.*

His father never fully understood the joys of battle or the nuance of warfare. The king of the gods preferred his women to more delightful pursuits. Mumbling a curse, Ares stopped before the massive gates of the city. He considered being polite and requesting an audience with Hector, prince of Troy, but he knew it would take too long. Instead, he opted for the faster route and snapped his fingers.

Hector appeared before him adorned only with a cloth that covered the lower half of his body. Ares took a moment to admire the Trojan's well-defined, furry pecs and abdomen. His full beard and piercing blue-grey eyes lent a strong majesty to a battle-hardened visage.

The moment Hector laid eyes on the god of war, he fell to one knee, clapped his right fist to his heart, and bowed his head. Ares moved to stand over the bronze-fleshed mortal and rested his hand on Hector's short-cropped black hair.

"I have need of you," Ares said.

"I serve you," Hector said. "What would you have me do, Lord?"

Ares pulled him to his feet and embraced him. Without urging, Hector pressed his lips to Ares's lips and pulled the god closer. Ares pushed his tongue into Hector's mouth and ripped away the cloth cinched at his waist. Already the Trojan's dick had hardened and pressed into Ares's thigh.

Reluctantly, Ares pulled away and said, "We must meet with Achilles."

"May I be permitted to ask why?" Hector asked.

Ares snapped his fingers, and they disappeared.

†††

Hector appeared, alone, inside the darkened confines of an opulent tent. Thick rugs covered the hard-packed ground. Various spears, swords, and shields leaned against the few chairs and a table that stood near the opening. An empty bed more befitting a king than a warrior butted up against a far corner.

A sword slid slowly in front of Hector's throat. He knew if he hadn't been disoriented by Ares's method of transportation, he would have realized the soldier was behind him well before he did. Slowly, Hector lifted his empty hands out to the side.

"What is a prince of Troy doing in my tent?"

"Lord Ares sent me, Achilles. Believe me, this was not my idea." Hector stiffened when he felt Achilles's hand on his cock, but the surprise quickly passed, and he leaned his head back, resting it on Achilles's shoulder. "It has been too long, my friend."

Achilles tossed the sword onto a rug. With his hand free, he grabbed Hector's throat, pulled the prince's head back a bit farther, and pressed their lips together. Hector reached back and grabbed onto Achilles's bare ass. He smiled into the kiss.

"Are you certain you were not expecting me?" he asked.

Achilles pushed him toward a nearby chair and fell backward into one himself. Hector turned and sat. He splayed one leg over a padded wooden arm and adjusted himself. Achilles lit an oil lamp and set it back on the table.

Hector had always admired the Greek warrior. They had trained together when they were younger, and Achilles's V-shaped torso still proved the envy of the known world. At least to Hector it did. Achilles's smooth chest and abdomen set atop legs that the Colossus of Rhodes would pine after. He had pulled his blond-brown hair back and bound it with a strip of leather. Sweat glistened from his muscles.

"Speak, Hector. We may be friends, but we are at war, and I am having a difficult time convincing myself I should not claim you as my captive," Achilles said.

Before Hector could reply, Ares appeared between them. "I sent him, Achilles. Not to be captured, but rather to do battle." Ares pulled his red cloak from his shoulders, and it disappeared, leaving him as naked as the two warriors who had fallen on their knees at his feet. Ares rubbed a hand over the short black hair covering his chest and twisted one of his nipples. At the same time he tugged on his growing erection.

"It is time for this war to end," Ares said. "I have decided that since it began with a competition, it will end with one, too. You and Achilles will engage in a battle, and to the victor will be given the means to win this war." He pulled both men to their feet.

"Will you provide weapons and armor, my Lord?"

"You already have the only weapon you need." Ares wrapped his hand around Hector's cock and gave it a slow stroke downward. He collected a single drop of nectar on his finger and then licked it clean. "Are you willing?"

"I live to serve you and Troy, Lord Ares." Hector said.

"And what of you, Achilles?" Ares repeated his motions with the Greek.

"I live to serve you, Lord Ares."

"Excellent. The victory conditions are simple: if you spill your seed, you lose," Ares said. He snapped his fingers, and the contents of the tent disappeared. A throne of skulls with daggers set into the ends of the armrests as ears replaced the missing furnishings. A cat pelt stretched across the entirety of the floor. Ares sat and slowly stroked himself; he nodded his consent to begin.

Hector wasted no time. Dropping to his knees, he grasped Achilles's cock at the base and slowly dragged his tongue up and over the head. He felt Achilles's fingers entwine his hair, and after a few more teasing licks, he opened wide. The thick shaft glided over his tongue. He sucked more in, felt the head pressing at the back of his throat. Hector retreated back to the head.

"You have no hope of winning this," Achilles said. He leaned over the top of Hector and pressed his finger between ass cheeks as hard as the walls of Troy themselves. Inexorably he pushed through Hector's defenses until he found the prize. A gasp tore itself from his throat when Hector surged forward. The Trojan's nose pressed against Achilles, and his throat massaged the spasming erection.

Behind them Ares grunted. Achilles saw the god of war with his legs hooked behind the throne's dagger ears. He had scooted forward until his ass rested on the edge of the seat, and while one hand made long, slow strokes on his cock, the fingers of his other hand pressed into his exposed hole.

When he realized he could not wrap his fingers into Hector's hair well enough to grip, Achilles grabbed the Trojan's beard and pulled him back. "Let's put that mouth to some better use," he said.

Hector crawled across the cat skin toward Ares without resistance and buried his face into the god's cleft. His tongue darted out and drew wet circles around the tight ring. Gripping Ares's hips, Hector dove in with greater effort. He added a finger to his ministrations and smiled when Ares groaned and squirmed.

"If you intend...By the gods, Hector, your tongue is amazing!" Ares panted and put his hand at the back of the mortal's head to press him farther into his task. "If you intend to include me in the battle, we must alter the victory conditions. The current rules stand." He gasped when Achilles began sucking on his pre-come-slick cock. "However, you may also win if you make me come."

Hector added a second finger to the god's ass. If Ares wanted to come, he would be happily obliged. He spit into his own palm several times and used it and his own pre-come to lube his dick. Pushing Achilles to the side, he moved into position and pressed his erection to Ares's quivering hole. They locked eyes, and Hector pushed forward.

The head of his cock pressed inside the tight ring, and Ares gasped. At the exact moment Ares adjusted to the invasion, Hector moved forward and pulled Ares's hips toward him at the same time. Both god and mortal threw their heads back in unison; their moans filled the tent.

Achilles backed away to watch his friend and patron joining together. He stroked himself and moved behind Hector. Just as Hector knew Achilles could be brought to climax through oral pleasure, Achilles knew Hector's weakness lay through being filled. Once in position, he grasped the back of Hector's neck, bent him over Ares, and pushed into Hector's ass.

With Ares's cock pressed into his abdomen, Hector bit Ares's neck and screamed his pain and pleasure into the god's flesh. Achilles pushed him so far forward that he could not draw back from Ares, so he settled for remaining deeply seated within the welcoming confines of Ares's inner sanctum.

Achilles knew Hector would not be able to hold out much longer. He had placed himself in the precarious position of being at the mercy of Achilles, and Achilles intended to press the advantage. With his hand still on Hector's neck, the Greek warrior began short, rapid strokes. He leaned down a bit to give himself better access to that spot within Hector that drove him insane with lust and battered away at it with abandon.

"By the gods, Achilles, stop," Hector panted. He struggled to push the man off of his back, but the waves of ecstasy pulsing throughout his entire body left him near the point of collapse. His willpower and restraint were flagging, and he knew he wouldn't be able to resist much longer. Attempts to clench his ass onto Achilles's cock proved fruitless. Achilles would not be thwarted.

"Come, Hector. Fill the god of war's ass with your seed and give me Troy," Achilles commanded.

"Never." Hector tried once more to stop the inevitable.

Ares looked into Hector's eyes and saw the defeat within them. "There is no shame in losing."

"But my people."

"I will see that the army is as merciful as possible," Achilles promised.

"No." Hector laid his head on Ares's chest. "Please, Achilles, no."

"Yes." Achilles willed himself to continue the onslaught although he could feel his strength waning. If he gave up now, he would never push Hector over the edge. As it was it took all his willpower to stem the tide of his seed.

Hector's scream drowned out the sounds of sweaty flesh and moans. He pushed himself as far as he could go into Ares's ass and unleashed a torrent of come. His legs shook like a battlefield trod by thundering hooves.

Within seconds of victory, Achilles loosed one volley into Hector's ass, and then he withdrew and sprayed the remainder of his seed onto the Trojan's back. Spent, he crumpled onto his back on the floor, his chest heaving. Come oozed from his slowly softening cock.

Hector succumbed to fatigue and fell onto his ass. He turned partially to lie across Achilles's heaving chest and pressed his lips to Achilles's lips.

"Remember your promise," Hector said.

"Neither of you will remember anything other than engaging in a great battle," Ares said. He stood over his finest acolytes, furiously jerking his cock, and sprayed them with his come. The earth shook beneath them all for several seconds.

Shaking the last drops from his dick, Ares told Hector, "You will remember to remove your loved ones from Troy. If you fail to do so, you will all perish." He knelt beside Hector, kissed him gently on the lips, and then snapped his fingers. Hector disappeared.

"I know we are at war, Lord Ares, but must the Trojan's perish?"

"Do not go weak on me at the climax, Achilles." Ares rubbed his dick over Achilles's lips and watched the warrior lick it clean. "I will spare Hector for today. You will return to the beach where the Greek army made landfall. I have arranged for Poseidon to give you a gift. Use it tonight and end this war. If you do not, I cannot be held responsible for what Zeus will do."

With a final kiss, Ares snapped his fingers and disappeared.

Achilles looked down at his come-drenched body, unsure how he had found himself in that state. He wrapped himself in a cloth lying nearby. The delicate fabric reminded him of one he had seen around the waist of Hector before it became a discarded casualty of their lovemaking. Dismissing the thought, he left his tent to find the rest of the army. A compulsion to go to the beachhead urged him into the waning light of the day.

In the distance he thought he could see the massive head of a wooden horse.

31

Leader of the Pack

By Logan Zachary

Coach Erik stood in the locker room looking into the full length mirror. His body glistened with sweat as he turned from side to side to see his body, still tight and hard after all of these years of coaching. His stomach was flat and his hips were narrow. His upper body made an impressive triangle up to his thick bull neck. His nostrils flared as he inhaled his musky male scent, and his gold ring wiggled back in forth with the breath. He turned his head to check out his profile and smiled. Head like a bull, nine inch horns, and hung like one too, even bigger. His hands caressed over the blunt rounded ends of the horns and worked down his torso to his massive member.

His bare feet padded on the damp tiled floor to the shower room. All the students had left for the day and now it was his time to shower and head home. The white tiled room echoed with his footfalls. His tight ass flexed with each step. The university paid him well, and his students loved him, but that did little to ease his loneliness.

He turned on the water and the hot spray washed over him. He lathered up with Minotaur Body Wash, strong enough for a bull, sexy enough for a man.

The exotic scents of Vanilla, Cedar wood, and Patchouli tingled his nose and made him inhale deeply. He had a long work out with the students and even ran the three-mile cool down. The water pressure, sharp against his skin, pounded his sore muscles, relaxing the tension they carried.

He soaped up his torso and the thick pelt of hair that descended to his pubic bush. His fingers combed through the soft hair. It looked coarse and curly, but was actually fine as a child's hair. The thick cream flowed over his semi-hard cock and over his low hanging balls. He stroked his dick and the lather foamed up even more. He scrubbed under his sack and pulled the heavy orbs up and rolled them in his hand.

His arousal grew as he moaned. He released his balls and reached behind him to wash his hairy crack. His fingers rode over the rock hard ass and dug deep into the crease, searching for the tender pink bud buried inside. He arched his back and let his finger play over the pucker and soap up his hole. He slowly slipped it inside and lathered it up.

He closed his eyes and stroked his cock with one hand as he fingered his tight butt. He turned to face the shower spray and opened his mouth wide to drink the hot water. He swallowed hard and slowly opened his eyes to see three pair of youthful eyes staring at him.

Aaron, Darren, and Taren Wilson watched him. The Wilson werewolf triplets were the hottest students on the football team. Muscular, hairy, handsome, and hung, just like their father.

Coach Erik quickly turned his back to the boys and grabbed for his towel. "What are you guys doing here?" His voice was angry as he wrapped the towel around his soapy waist. His huge arousal made it hard to cover himself with the too small towel.

"We forgot our towels and workout clothes. Tonight is wash night." Aaron said and then bit his lower lip. His hand mindlessly adjusted himself in his sweatpants. He was free balling and his business grew under his touch.

Darren's mouth hung wide open, and Taren dropped his gym bag onto the tiled floor.

"Well, grab your things and get on home. I'm sure your father is expecting you." Coach Erik slowly turned, but stayed hunched over to cover his raging hard on as much as the thin towel allowed.

Aaron stepped into the shower room and stood in front of Coach. He reached forward and touched his coach's chest. "He'll wait, but I've never seen such fine muscular detail before." His hand slipped over the foamy pec and down to the erect nipple. The sharp point stuck into his palm, and his fingers involuntarily pinched and rolled the nub.

Coach Erik moaned and tried to cover his engorging groin even more, but his erection popped out of the slit in the cotton.

Aaron fell down on his knees, his sweats instantly soaked, but he didn't notice with the massive cock jumping in front of his face. He leaned forward and licked the fat uncut tip. A pearl of pre-come dripped out and landed on his tongue. He lapped it up and groaned with joy. He reached forward and pulled the Coach's narrow hips closer. He opened his mouth and swallowed the end of his dick. The spicy soap didn't prevent him. His tongue trailed along the veiny underside and sucked him in deeper.

There was a commotion behind Coach Erik, and then the next thing he knew, Darren and Taren stood buck ass naked and on either side of him. They caressed his biceps and worked down his forearms.

Coach Erik's excited hands dropped the towel into the shower's spray and thrust his hips forward.

Aaron swallowed another few inches before choking on his girth. He cupped the Coach's ass and pulled his cheeks apart and forward, driving him deeper into his throat. His finger found the pink pucker and teased it.

Coach Erik gasped, and his cock jerked in Aaron's mouth. "I'm your coach, you can't do this. I can't do this." But his body betrayed him, refusing to fight or flight.

Darren and Taren grabbed Coach's arms and pulled him down to the tiled floor. Aaron crawled up his legs as his tight ass hit the floor and helped pin Coach down. He spread his hairy legs and licked down his shaft.

Water washed over the men, and Aaron finally realized he was the only one dressed and quickly stripped as his lips sucked on the Coach's foreskin.

"Boys," he started, but his resistance refused to fight. Lick him, lick him.

"Coach, we're men, as if you haven't noticed." Darren moved closer to his face and dangled his dick over the Coach's mouth and traced his lips with the pink tip.

Coach Erik couldn't resist licking the slit as it rolled around his mouth. Salty sweet pre-come danced over his tongue and made his mouth water. He drew the dripping penis into his mouth and deep throated it, sucking as much of the sweet ambrosia from Darren as he could.

Taren sat on his arm and guided his fingers to his willing hole.

Coach explored the tight end and slipped his index finger inside. He wiggled it as the triplet rode his hand.

Taren rubbed one of his horns and stroked along the length of it. Waves of pleasure flowed through the calcified horn and flowed deep into Coach Erik's skull. His body bucked on the tiled floor and a bellow rose from deep down from his diaphragm echoed through the locker room.

"*Wait!*" he gasped as his nostrils flared and shot out snot. "I am the one who tells you what you guys do. So let me up and get dressed."

Aaron rose onto his knees and let Coach Erik's dick drop out of his mouth. He lifted a leg and exposed an ass cheek. He slapped it hard, making a red spot appear, and his hand stung from the impact on the wet skin. "We've listened to you on the field all season, but in the shower room, the rules are different. There are three against one, and we want something."

"What?" Coach Erik asked, before Darren slipped his dick back into his mouth.

"You. We want what you've been flashing in the mirror, your hot Minotaur body. You've ridden our ass all season and now the table has turned, you're our sex slave tonight. We want to ride your ass." Aaron slapped his ass again, this time leaving a hand print on his hairy cheek.

Darren pulled his cock out of Coach's mouth, crawled to his gym bag, and pulled something out. The metallic item clinked on the tiles. Shackles. He tossed one to Taren before he secured one of Coach Erik's wrists to the water pipe.

Taren mirrored his actions a few seconds later.

Aaron climbed on top of Coach's pelvis. His hairy ass slide over his coach's uncut cock and trapped it between his gluts. His buns of steel squeezed as it slid along its girth, pulling the foreskin back and forth over the bull sized dick.

Coach Erik pulled hard with all of his might against the restraints, but couldn't budge them. He was trapped. "Now, boys, fun is fun, but …"

"Yes, let's talk about butts." Darren stood and turned his back to Coach.

Taren did the same thing. Two beautiful, young hairy werewolf asses loomed over their fearless leader.

Coach Erik closed his eyes and lay back on the floor. He had dreamed about this kind of thing happening many times, but he never thought it ever would. "This can't be happening, this can't be happening," he kept repeating to himself.

Then he stopped. He inhaled deeply and licked his lips. He thought he felt something tickle his nose. He opened his eyes and Darren's ass was straddling his face. His balls swung back and forth over Coach's snout, the musky male ball sweat teased his taste buds.

His tongue fell out of his mouth and swiped at the heavy sack. A few coarse bristles tickled his tongue before being pulled away.

Darren's pink pucker winked at him.

Taren laughed as he moved behind Darren, spooning his brother's body so two dicks swung over their Coach's face. "I've always wanted to do this." He sat down on the Coach's face. He spread his cheeks and guided his hairy hole over their captive's mouth. "Lick me." His balls flopped over Coach's nose as he relaxed his butt.

Coach Erik couldn't resist any longer. He licked the pucker and swirled his tongue around and around. He rolled and lapped at the bud, drilling the opening and trying to taste deeper.

Taren threw his head back and howled. His legs twitched like a dog being scratched.

His brothers howled with him, the pack training unable to override their sneaky attack.

Aaron bounced on his dick and could feel it pulsate underneath him. He tapped his brothers back. "Huddle up."

Taren reluctantly stood and stepped away.

Darren didn't waste the wagging tongue. He offered his ass for his tongue bath, but got more than he bargained for as the talented sensory organ entered his backside. He felt his balls rise and threaten to empty across the Coach's face.

"Darren, don't you dare," Aaron scolded.

Reluctantly, Darren slow rose and tea bagged his sack into the open mouth. He arched his back to get them to drop in deeper and allow maximum tongue action.

"Darren," was all Aaron growled, and he snapped his fingers to hurry his brother along.

The three brothers circled each other and threw their arms around each other as they spoke in hushed tones.

Coach Erik strained to hear what they were planning next, but couldn't hear the brother's plan.

"Break," the three said in unison and clapped their hands. As they turned back to their coach, they saw his legs were up and over his head, trying to push against the wall, but it only opened his ass up to them.

"Look what we have here," Aaron said. "I never thought of the Coach as a bottom, but if he is opening up to us ..." he let his words hang in the steamy air.

The shower continued to spray over his body.

Taren opened his gym bag and pulled out his cell phone. He found the camera and snapped some beautiful pictures of their bound Coach. His hairy butt filled the screen.

"Get a few shots of his huge dick and make sure you get his beautiful face in there. We want to give the right man all the credit he deserves."

"This could get me fired." Coach Erik flopped on his back on the floor and his hard on stood straight up, proud and happy.

"This year's student annual will have a centerfold," Darren said. He moved over and knelt down so his penis was across Coach's mouth. He stroked it a few times and pre-come dripped out of the tip. "Come on, lick it."

Coach Erik took a deep breath and said, "At least, I'll go out with a bang."

"That you will," Aaron said. "I think we need to show you who's the boss?" He motioned for Taren to grab a leg. He moved between his legs and searched for his hole with his dick.

Darren grabbed his other leg. "Aaron, you're first."

"Wait, wait, wait." Coach Erik pulled on his arm shackles as he felt his legs spread open wider. His hairy hole puckered as Aaron's cock slipped around and around, seeking entry. "I'm your coach. You need to listen to me."

Aaron looked down at him and smiled. His dick pressed against his opening. "Who's in control?" His dick slipped in a little as he increased the pressure. He reached forward and stroked Coach's cock and could feel the sphincter relax and allow him to sink deeper in. Aaron moaned from the wonderful feeling. He pushed in deeper and worried his balls would release if he went any further. "You need to give us what we want."

Coach Erik felt him go in deeper and wanted more. He pressed against him and felt Aaron sink in deeper. "Anything you want." He couldn't deny them anything at this point.

Darren and Taren looked at each other and waited as Aaron slid back and forth. They knew what he wanted and what they wanted. But who could deny the pleasure he was experiencing right now?

Aaron closed his eyes and moaned as he slowly withdrew from the perfect butt. "Anyone else want to try it? Because I'm gonna blow my wad soon."

Taren nodded and switched places with Aaron. He licked the hairy hole teasing it with his tongue before he stuck his dick in. He humped the Coach's rump a few times and pulled out. He slapped a cheek. "God, you are amazing." He wiped his ooze from the tip of his cock before taking Darren's place.

Darren fingered the hairy opening, as if he was checking the seal. He wiggled his finger around and stroked his dick before slipping it in. Inch by inch he slowly sunk in and as soon as his pubic bush touched Coach Erik's ass, he shuddered. An expression of bliss came over his face as he rocked back and forth.

"You fucker, you came," Aaron said. He let go of Coach's leg.

Darren pumped a few more times into Coach and pulled out as Aaron touched him. His dick dripped on the tiled floor, a huge splat of come. "I reload quickly, you know that."

Aaron tapped him on his shoulder. "No self-control."

Taren laughed as he let go of the leg he was holding. "Come on and release him."

The triplets let their leader go, unchaining his arms. Coach Erik rubbed the circulation back into his sore arm muscles. As the blood returned, so did his massive erection. His gaze went from one werewolf to the next and the next, enjoying the rippling muscles, the patterns of hair and the variety of dicks. They surrounded him and caressed his body, six hands covering every nerve ending on him.

Coach Erik shuddered as his body responded. The spicy scent of his soap, mixed with the animal musk of sex, testosterone, and ball sweat. He inhaled deeply, savoring the intoxicating aroma. He knew he would never be able to enter the locker room again with a raging hard on. This memory was burned into his mind forever and hotwired to his dick.

"We want you in us," Aaron whispered into his ear. He nibbled on his ear lobe and slipped his tongue deep inside the canal.

The wet, warm tongue tickled him, making him giggle like a school girl. He twisted his neck to escape, but he didn't struggle hard. Darren tongued his other ear, as Taren kissed him full on. Hands entered his crease, down to his hole, a hand cupped his balls and squeezed, fingers pinched his nipples, entered his ass, slid all over his beautiful body. His knees felt weak, unable to hold him any longer.

""Let move to the wrestling mat," Aaron said as he pulled the bull by his balls.

Coach Erik willing followed, his cock dripping all the way. The three never removed their hands from his body, not in fear of his escape, but inability to stop. "What do you want?" he said into Taren's mouth. Their tongues tangled before another kiss deepened.

They lowered him to the mat and Aaron took the lead. He straddled the Coach's lap and slid along his cock.

Pre-come flowing out of his foreskin, as he asked, "How can I be inside all of you?"

"We have an idea," Taren said as he kissed his willing mouth.

Aaron guided his body to welcome the uncut cock. He rocked his hips as Darren stood behind him, pinching his pecs and massaging his chest to relax him to allow his ass to relax enough to accommodate the Coach's girth.

The hooded head was slippery, lubed by nature and soak entry. Coach Erik didn't need to think, his body worked on pure instinct, pure animal lust. The four bodies slid and rode over and over each other, where one started and one ended didn't matter, they all were one.

Aaron arched his back as the fat tip entered him. He felt his hole stretch like it never did before at his tender age. He held still, allowing the pain to slowly turn into pleasure.

His brothers sensed his discomfort and turned their attention to his body to distract his pain and relax. The mushroom head popped in and the pain stopped. He sat still, held in place by the ball of writhing flesh. Slowly, his butt relaxed, and he slid down the bull's dick. Once the coach was inside of him, he nodded to his brothers. They slowly receded from Aaron and focused their affection on Coach. They moved along his body and thrust their junk into his hands. The Coach never fumbled a ball in his life and he didn't now with the most perfect ones rolling between his fingers.

Aaron started to slowly ride his cock and massage along his torso. "The boys want you inside them too." He circled his navel and combed along his treasure trail.

"I only have one," he started to say until he felt the other brothers' hands stroke along each of his horns. The thrill sent waves of electricity over his body. All the hair on his body stood on end, and the caresses rocked his skull, thumping with every beat of his heart.

Taren and Darren stroked their cocks to milk out their own pre-come and applied the clear fluid over their Coach's horns. They lubed the rounded tips of horns till they shone and glided smoothly in their palm.

"But how?"

"We got it." Darren turned on his knees and aimed his beautiful ass at the glistening horn. He reached back and guided the smooth tip to his hole and inserted it. The narrow end entered easily and Darren slowly back up, feeling the horn grow in girth as it drilled in deeper. He rounded the slight curve and groaned with pleasure.

Coach could smell the man's ball musk and felt his cock swell inside of Aaron.

Aaron moaned as he felt it too.

"How is it?" Taren asked.

"Better than we ever thought," Darren cooed. "Hurry up, I can't take much more. I want him to pound my ass."

"Me too," Aaron echoed.

Taren lubed his hairy hole and repeated his brother's actions. He left a trail of pre-come across the mat as he impaled himself on the Coach's horn. He felt Darren's foot as he hit the reverse curve and knew he was there. "Oh yeah," was all he could say as he pressed back on the horn.

Aaron started to move up and down as he rode the Coach. "Oh, yeah."

Darren rocked back and forth on his hands and knees, moving only a little at first. He felt the Coach's head rock with him. The horn moved in and out, filling him and relaxing. "This is fucking fantastic. We should have done this so long ago."

Taren joined in, matched his motion with the rhythm and pace of his brother.

Coach let his head bounce back and forth between the boys' butts. He could feel the warm, wet pressure that pulsated over his horn. He never realized how many nerve fibers he had in his horns; they were quickly becoming his new plaything. He thrust his hips up and slammed into Aaron, taking him by surprise.

Aaron gasped as his prostate was tapped and almost shot his load. He stroked his cock as he rode Coach. He moaned and groaned, enjoying the view of his brothers' asses being plugged. The power he felt made him giddy with joy. He stroked harder as he saw Darren and Taren rise and fall on the horns. The scent of sex filled the room covering the usual odor of bleach and damp moldy smell of the locker room.

Coach Erik closed his eyes and let his head bob with the boys. He let the pleasure rise over his body. He floated for a while as the warmth spread over him. As the motion increased, he felt he could join in, increasing his pace and depth as they moved with him and against him. Time seemed to speed up and slow down. He could see every minute detail and savored every second.

The triplets fell into a rhythm, they arched their backs, and their moans synchronized into howls.

Coach Erik was in a surround sound of sex, hair, asses, and throbbing cocks. Pre-come flowed over everyone and everywhere. The sensation increased as well as their need for more, deeper, faster, harder. The male sex smell burned his olfactory nerves as his skin tingled with each touch.

Darren reached over with his free hand and took Taren's. As their fingers curled around each other, a brotherly bound increased and they knew it wouldn't be long. Aaron saw the glow between his brothers and reached forward and touched their asses. There was a crackle of static electricity, and the room hummed with energy as the triangle was completed.

Another howl broke out between the brothers and echoed throughout the locker room.

Coach Erik felt the power too and increased his thrusts.

Darren jacked hard and sat back as an arc of come shot out of his dick, spraying over the mat. Spurt after spurt shot out of him.

As soon as the scent of the hot load entered Taren's nose, he inhaled deeply and his balls shot the eruption he had been holding back. Rope after rope of come splattered over Coach Erik's face.

Coach licked his lips and drew the young man's seed into his mouth. The salty sweet triggered his climax and unloaded his balls into Aaron.

Aaron felt the volcano explode and fill his ass. His prostate gland throbbed and sent out its own gush of come, covering Coach Erik's torso. Their bodies throbbed and pounded as a collective orgasm hit them all at once. Darren and Taren screamed, as Aaron fell back and Coach Erik tensed up, unable to move in fear that his body would explode as his cock had just done.

The men collapsed in a doggie pile and huddled together as their sweat and semen flowed and mixed together.

The brothers lay across their coach and basked in the warmth. Their fluids dripped around them and formed a pool of semen and sweat underneath.

After their breathing returned to normal, one by one the brothers sat up and massaged their hairy leader's body.

He just moaned and enjoyed the attention. "We should hit the shower." Coach slapped Aaron's ass.

"Isn't that where all of this started?" he asked.

The four headed back to the shower and washed each other. Foam flowed over their hairy bodies and washed them clean, refreshing their energy and re-awakened their arousals.

"The janitor will be here soon, so we need to get our hairy asses out of here." Coach Erik walked bare assed to the shelf for a new dry towel. He was no longer modest with his athletes. He grabbed a few more towels and tossed one to each brother. He saw the soaked sweats on the floor and picked up a pair of gym shorts and a T-shirt. Once he was dry, he waited for Aaron to finish. "Here," he said and threw the clothes to him.

Aaron stepped into the dry shorts, and the outline of his huge dick revealed his thick cut penis in all of its glory.

"You may have a little trouble getting home," Coach said as he pointed to the bulge.

Darren and Taren waved him off. "That's nothing new."

Aaron turned and flashed his ass as the material hugged his hairy butt as if a second skin.

"I'm going to have a hard time getting home," Coach Erik said as his dick rose to full mast.

Darren and Taren finished dressing and stared at their Coach's dick.

"Coach Erik, do you want to come over and use our hot tub? We can order pizza, and I know we have cold beer in the refrigerator." Aaron looked like a little boy asking for a puppy.

How could he say no to those big brown eyes? Coach Erik wondered.

But before he could say anything, Darren said, "And Daddy has a dungeon downstairs."

Coach Erik looked into the locker room mirror. He didn't need big brown eyes to answer that one.

The Curse of Glen Connor

By Gio Lassater

While Arklow hadn't been one of my intended destinations traveling through Ireland, the fact that I stumbled upon the Seabreeze Festival made me glad I'd changed my mind. A street fair with lots of music, food, and people who wanted nothing more than to have a good time made the detour worthwhile.

Unfortunately, my arrival coincided with the end of the festival, but the fireworks display was spectacular. After a full day of taking in everything, I decided to have a relaxing night. I wandered along Main Street, enjoying the breeze, the sounds of continuing revelry, and the architecture of a city that had been around since the Viking invasions.

When I spotted The Old Ship pub, I knew I had found my destination. Inside, the lights were low, and the crowd was thin. Only a few people sat at the bar or among the tables scattered throughout the room. Some peace and quiet would settle me for the night.

I paid for my pint of house ale and meandered around a jumble of chairs until I reached a table in a back corner. When I sat my backpack on the floor a cloud of dust puffed into the air. Waving it away, I plopped onto a hardwood chair and took a big drink.

By the time I had worked my way through most of the pint, the lack of noise and stimulation in addition to the alcohol had relaxed me to the point I had almost started dozing off. I could feel my eyelids drooping—a clear sign it was time to find a room or a park somewhere to crash.

Gulping down the last bit of ale, I grabbed my pack and had just started standing when a man walked through the front door. Our eyes locked for a brief moment, but that was enough to stop me in mid-motion. Leaning over the table like a criminal in the stocks, I stared at him, forcing my mouth to remain closed. He nodded once and continued on his way to the bar.

I sat back down, unable to take my eyes off of him. His clothes said that he was probably a day laborer of some sort, but his demeanor and the way he carried himself bespoke a pride that drew attention away from the threadbare nature of his attire. Reddish-brown hair peeked from beneath a grey-striped ivy cap. The well-trimmed beard and mustache matched his hair color, and the brief look I had of his sapphire eyes set my heart off at a marathon pace.

Even in the near silence of the pub I couldn't hear his voice when he ordered. The bartender's smile mirrored the feelings stirring in my pants, and when he set the glass in front of the handsome stranger, he briefly touched the man's fingers. Blushing, the barman hurriedly turned away and busied himself at the other end of the bar.

The man gave no indication he noticed the bartender's reaction. I hoped he would sit close to me, but he opted to take the farthest table away. Luckily he sat where I could see his face and imagine myself melting into his arms.

"Do you want another one?"

I dragged my gaze from the stranger's face and looked up at the barmaid. She smiled as if she knew what thoughts had been running through my head. Nodding dumbly, I handed her my empty glass and forgot about her until she returned with another pint and a wink.

The man didn't do much beside drink from the dark liquid he'd ordered. Occasionally he would run a finger absentmindedly around the rim of the glass, but for the most part he sat staring into space. To me he didn't appear to be sad or preoccupied. He looked content and unhurried. Peaceful. Those were my first impressions.

However, once I had spent some time really watching him—not just drooling over the thoughts of what I would enjoy doing to him—I noticed his shoulders hunched forward, and he occasionally sighed for no reason. When the bar maid brought him another drink without asking, he didn't acknowledge her. She didn't seem fazed by the treatment. I got the feeling he was a regular, and this was a common occurrence.

I don't know whether it was the alcohol or desire that finally stiffened my resolve, but before I could talk myself out of it, I grabbed my pack and made my way toward his table. When I stopped a few feet from him, it felt like electricity crackled in the air around me. He had a presence that drew me in, but at the same time I felt like I was being pushed away from him by some unseen force.

"Um, excuse me," I said after a few awkward seconds of not being noticed. He looked up at me, and I licked my lips and cleared my throat in an attempt to find my suddenly cowardly voice. "Um, hi. I'm not from here, and I was wondering if you could tell me where I might find a place to rest tonight."

One corner of his mouth quirked up in a half smile that I knew held some sadness. "American?" he asked.

"I am," I said. "Are you from around here? You don't sound Irish."

He grunted. "You're not the first person to tell me that. People have a habit of hearing what they want to when they're around me. It's part of my curse."

"I didn't mean to upset you. Sorry for bothering you." I started to walk away.

"Wait, mate, I didn't mean to be gruff. Have a seat. I'll order you a pint to make up for my attitude." He stood and indicated the chair across from his own. "Please. I wouldn't want your experience in Arklow to be overshadowed by the one rude bastard you ran into." His voice, so melodic and disarming, drew me back, and I gladly accepted the invitation.

"My name is Destry," I said. When his hand touched mine, it felt like the imagined electricity in the air coalesced in the palm of his hand. I found myself unable to let go as I stared at him like a love-sick teenager.

He acted as if he didn't notice. "Destry. Like the movie?"

I blushed and nodded, finally remembering to release his hand. "Yeah, my dad was a big Jimmy Stewart fan. I happened to be unlucky enough to be his only son, so I got stuck with the name from his favorite movie."

"I like it. My name's Glen, by the way. Glen Connor. It's a pleasure to meet you," he said.

"For me too. I didn't mean to interrupt you. If you want to be alone, I can ask someone else about a room," I said.

He waved away my concern and held up two fingers toward the bartender. "Don't think on it, mate. Have a drink with me to make up for my rude behavior, and then I can show you a good place to pass the night away."

Within an hour I had downed several pints, and I had told Glen about every aspect of my life. I'd never had such an easy time talking about myself before, but there was something about him that put me at ease. I'm sure the alcohol didn't hurt that, either.

An ancient clock on the wall chimed midnight. I looked from it to my near-empty glass. When my gaze shifted back to Glen, his sparkling eyes stared so deeply into me that I felt I could get lost in them for eternity.

"What sort of accommodations were you thinking about?" he asked after draining his glass.

"Well, since I wasn't actually planning to come here, I don't really have anywhere particular in mind. I saw a place on my map called

Abbey Park. I thought I might camp out under the stars tonight," I said.

Glen chuckled. "You might want to rethink that plan, mate. Abbey Park is a cemetery."

I laughed and downed the last drink in my glass. "Yeah, I think I'll skip that, thanks. You have any suggestions?"

"Most places are booked up due to the festival." He stood up and pulled on his ivy cap. "If you don't mind a couch, you can stay at my place. Mind, I don't normally have visitors, so the place is a bit rough."

"I've seen worse, I'm sure." I stood up and wobbled sideways. "Damn, that sneaks up on ya, doesn't it?"

He laughed and came around to slip an arm across my shoulders. "Indeed it does. Let me help you."

I put my arm around his back, holding him tightly, and let him steer me toward the door. My body tingled the entire length where I touched him, and his hand felt warm like an inviting fire on a cold night. By the time we stumbled through the door into the street, I had grown accustomed to the warmth. I wasn't looking forward to him letting me go.

† † †

Glen led me toward the river, regaling me with tales about its various names throughout the years. Unfortunately it was so polluted that nobody could swim in it anymore, but the way he spoke so fondly of it, I could tell he felt a connection with it.

After walking for a ways out of the town, I realized we had left civilization behind. My mind had started to unfuzzy itself, and I feared that I had willingly and wantonly put myself into the hands of a man who intended to murder me in the middle of nowhere.

"Maybe I should find a place in town," I said.

Glen stopped walking and leaned his head close until his lips were mere centimeters from my ear. "Do you really want that? If you do, I'll not stop you. It's just that you've been fawning over me so much tonight that I thought you had some fun in mind for tonight."

The wind suddenly shifted, encircling us in a whirlwind of leaves and flowers that glinted in the soft white light of the moon. It felt like the whole world had disappeared and we were the center of the universe. Chills ran through my body, and when I saw a sparkle in Glen's eyes, I felt like Alice falling down the rabbit hole.

My lips pressed against his before I realized I intended to kiss him. He tasted of spring and bliss. I could inexplicably smell rain even though the sky was cloudless. His hands covered my ears, and he brought me in, kissing me so deeply that I had the falling sensation again.

"You are mine, Destry."

"Yes." I kissed him, shoving my tongue into his mouth. My hands grabbed his waist, forcing our hips together. Still the wind blew, swirled around us. The night felt like it was on fire, but I realized it was the heat Glen gave off.

"You are mine," he said again. "Mine."

The wind died. My vision blurred, and a door closed. When I could see properly again, we stood in the center of a small room in what I was sure was a quaint Irish cottage. How we had arrived there—when neither of us had moved—I didn't know, but I soon forgot all my questions about everything.

"Undress. Slowly," Glen said. His voice had a soft lilt to it that made me weak in the knees.

Glen sank into a high-backed, plush chair that appeared behind him. He tossed a leg over the arm of the chair, rubbing his obviously hard cock in slow circles through his breeches. I began to undo the buttons of my shirt, one by one, waiting until Glen nodded before proceeding to the next one. With the last one freed, I slowly pulled the two panels of the shirt apart.

"Very nice," Glen said. He leaned forward, running his hands up the smooth skin of my stomach. His fingers played along the ridges of my abs and rubbed circles around my hard nipples. Dragging the back of his hand from my neck to my crotch, he cupped my cock, squeezing.

"You may continue," he said.

I kicked my shoes off and unbuttoned my pants at the same time. Glen admonished me when I started to rush, but I couldn't help it. I was hot and horny, and the thought of having him on me, in me, drove me insane. If he didn't touch me, I'd lose my mind!

"Breathe, Destry. Soon. I promise." The fact he echoed my thoughts with his words was uncanny.

With my thumbs hooked inside the waistline of my pants, I shifted from side to side, dragging the denim over my hips, down my thighs, past my knees, to my ankles. Since I hadn't worn underwear that day, I stood naked before him.

He indicated I should turn around. His hand caressed the hard mounds of my ass, massaging them, prying them apart. He smacked my cheeks, rubbing his palm in circles to ease the sting.

Almost as if I could sense what he desired, I leaned forward, resting my hands on the cushions of a rustic couch. Glen's thumb traveled up and down the cleft of my ass, rubbing over my hole, pressing against it. When I tried to thrust backward he slapped my ass, hard.

"Bad boys don't get their way."

"I'm sorry." And I truly was. The thought that he might stop and refuse to give me what I so desperately needed—him!—filled my stomach with dread. "Please, Glen, don't stop. I'll be good. I promise."

"See that you are. That was your only warning." He kissed where he slapped and continued circling my hole with his thumb. It seemed like that's all he did for an eternity. Like he was testing my resolve to see if I'd hold out or if I couldn't help but give in and try to force him inside me.

But I knew that if I did that, he'd stop, and I'd die. I had to have him. That had never happened before, not with any man I've ever had.

Glen was unique—the epitome of sex and sexy—and my heart would burst if I didn't take what he had to give.

When Glen stopped and sat back, I'm sure I groaned, but not from pleasure. This was torture. He needed to fuck me!

"Patience." He spoke to my thoughts again. "Turn around." I did as he commanded—far more quickly than I probably should have. He pulled his pants down.

I immediately thought that I'd never be able to take all of him, followed by the determination to do my damnedest to do exactly that. There was no doubt it would hurt, but I couldn't care less. I needed him. *I needed him.* I stopped myself before I said that aloud.

Glen smacked his ample girth against his stomach. A line of precome trailed from his perfect abs to the tip of his delicious cock. He moved down in the chair, hooking a leg over each arm of the chair, waving his erection at me. Light glinted off a dollop of sweet nectar at the tip; I wanted to lick it clean.

"I like that you comply so well," Glen said. His smile was bright, and I felt my knees go weak.

I knelt before him, licking my lips while I contemplated the hard piece of flesh he taunted me with. A single nod was all I required. My tongue swiped the drop of precome, and I savored the sweet taste. I knew I couldn't fit all of him into my mouth, so I focused on the head. I bathed it, dragging my tongue in swirls and circles. I pulled it into my mouth, sucking more and more of the shaft in.

My mouth was full, stretched wide, and I realized I had barely made any progress. His girth was phenomenal. His balls, so heavy with the come I wanted to milk from him, rubbed against my palm. Moving from his cock, I took first one into my mouth and then the other and covered them with my spit.

Glen watched me service him. His finger trailed through my spit on the way to his ass. I knew I wouldn't be inside him, but the thought that he was stimulating himself while I tried to force his monstrous cock into my throat was maddening.

My tongue traveled from his balls, down to the tight ring of flesh he teased. I darted my tongue along it. With both hands, Glen pulled his cheeks apart, giving me unfettered access. I pressed my tongue against him, lapping at it like a dog at water. Thrusting. Pressing. Groaning. I buried my face into his innermost areas and relished the ability to do so. The heat he generated intensified.

"Are you ready?" he asked.

In response, I turned around and crawled onto the couch. Leaning over the back, I thrust my ass into the air and spread myself open for him. His chuckle sent shivers through me. He moved behind me, gently prodding my hole over and over with the tip of his cock. Anticipation drove me insane. Again, I wanted to thrust backward and violate myself.

"I give you one last chance to end this before it's too late. I can still release you." The words danced in my ears.

"Please fuck me, Glen." Even I could hear the lust, desire, and need in my voice.

"You will never desire another man," he warned.

I looked back at him. Something the bartender said—something I inexplicably didn't remember until that very moment—screamed in my mind. *Stay away from that one. He'll be the end of you after just once in his bed.*

The room seemed to expand. Glen's cock still lay nestled in the cleft of my ass. He moved it back and forth, thrusting it slowly up and down. It felt as if the whole world anticipated my response.

"You're joking, right? This is just something you tell all the guys. Right?" My voice quivered.

"I tell this to every man, but none of them ever believe me," he said with a hint of sadness in his voice. "You must make the choice. If you say yes, I will show you a night of passion you will *never* forget. I guarantee it. If you say no, you will have saved yourself from my curse."

What? Curse? He had to be joking. The expression on his face was nothing but dead serious. I had to know. I had to know what having him inside me feels like.

"Do it."

The room suddenly came into such clear focus that I nearly passed out from the vibrancy. Colors jumped around like they did that one time I did acid in college. Glen smiled, and the glint in his eye sparkled again. The sound of rushing wind—like before we came inside—filled the room. Glen's heat spread over me.

I groaned, and he pressed forward, sweetly urging my defenses to lower, to let him inside.

Focus on breathing. In. Out. Let him in. Relax.

Oh, god!

My teeth sank into the cushion of the couch when the head of his cock popped inside me. He stopped moving, holding position. Soothing words. I heard them, but I couldn't understand what he said. They must have been Gaelic, but they did the trick. Warmth slowly replaced the pain. Soon, I felt nothing but a rushing euphoria.

"I won't hurt you." The promise rang true in my soul. "Give yourself to me, Destry. Allow my magic to work in you. You are mine. For this moment in time, I am yours."

Magic...

"Yes." The word fluttered from my lips and hung in the air above me. Glen pressed in. Stretched me. I understood why he said there would never be another. I would never feel this sensation again. So full. So tight. So. Fucking. Amazing!

Glen started talking in Gaelic again, still so soothing. I took a chance and pressed into him, just slightly, not enough to look like I was trying to take control. He gripped my hips, pulled. His speech became a chant, and before I even realized it, he had completely entered me.

I gasped and tried to move forward, but Glen's grip tightened and he thrust into me. My teeth bit into the cushion. He held me for the longest time, chanting. When silence filled the room, I experienced every inch—length and girth—of his cock. Unbelievable.

"Are you ready?"

No! "Yes."

He withdrew. I attempted to relax, but his retreat triggered my body's desire to have the foreign invader out of me. Glen thrust back in. I moaned into the couch. The motion repeated until I relaxed enough for him to pull out more and more. The sound of wind and heat continued to fill me and the room.

By the time Glen's cock moved completely in and out of me, I was begging him to fuck me. And I mean begging. He complied, thrusting into me, faster, deeper. The fabric of the couch scraped my knees raw. His fingers bruised my hips.

And yet he didn't relent.

My screams soon drowned out everything else. His massive cock rubbed my prostate into a state of frenzy. My warning that I was going to come didn't even reach my lips. I showered the couch, drenching my chest and the cushion near my face. I licked it clean, high on the heady scent of sex and the feeling of utter fulfillment.

Glen forced my head down, lifting my ass higher into the air, going at me like a jackhammer possessed by Satan. He whispered to me; I groaned and begged him not to stop.

His chanting resumed, and as he reached a crescendo, I felt liquid warmth filling my ass. Glen shouted, bottomed out inside me, and held me against him while his cock quivered and spasmed. I gulped air into my lungs, teetering on the precipice of consciousness and oblivion.

Come ran down my leg, and yet Glen did not stop.

Finally, he collapsed onto my back, kissed my neck, licked the outer edge of my ear, and whispered, "Goodbye, Destry."

††††

When I awoke to the sound of rushing water and the warmth of sunlight on my cheeks, the ache in my heart began immediately. I rolled onto my side and pushed myself to my feet. The smell of sex and dry come assaulted my nose, filling me with shame and desire.

"Glen?"

What was I doing on the bank of the river? Where was Glen's house? I'm naked...

"Glen, I need you. Glen, don't leave. Glen!" My shout echoed across the river. Tears streamed down my face, and I clutched at my chest.

"The glanconer got what he wanted," a man said, stepping from behind a tree nearby.

I was in too much pain to worry about covering myself. The man, I realized, was the bartender from the night before. The look on his face held comforting sadness. He extended his hand, offering me a thin blanket.

"What happened? And what's a glanconer?" I unfolded the blanket and wrapped it around my waist. Tears continued to fall, and I leaned back. No amount of air gulped into my lungs eased the sting in my heart.

"Damned fairy folk," he said. "The worst of the lot, if you ask me. He fucks ya, then he leaves ya. You'll never be the same, laddie. I'm sorry."

I fell on my ass, staring at the bartender, trying to make sense of his words. He couldn't be right. I would find Glen again. He would come back for me.

He had to.

He had to.

"Glen..."

Tribute

By V. Hummingbird

Raphael stood braced in the doorway of the shanty cabin, staring out into the rain. The night was deep, and still, save the constant sizzle of water through the trees. The dim glow of his gas lantern created a small circle of light out over the dampened pine needles, and he watched its edge with trepidation.

Any moment now and the creature would step into the glow.

Rivulets coursed down his arms and shoulders, making his thin gray t-shirt stick to his frame. He felt sticky, and overly warm, and wanted nothing more than to duck inside the shelter and strip down to nothing.

But he couldn't. Not yet. Not with that *thing* still out there.

A quick snap drew Raphael's attention to the left, and he hoisted his shotgun, finger poised above the trigger.

He'd caught a glimpse of it right before the sun went down. The thing was huge, but appeared human, save for its navy-blue skin, horse-like tail, and the two horned nubs on its temples. He thought perhaps its eyes were yellow, but he hadn't stuck around long enough to find out.

When it had seen him it let out a vicious growl. Not feral, like an animal, but distinctly *hungry*.

This couldn't be what he'd been sent out here to hunt, could it? They'd said there was a monster in the woods, but he thought perhaps it was a wolf, or a bear—game he'd taken before.

Not this.

Another snap, and a naked foot slid into the light, followed by a powerful male calf and thigh. It slipped into view slow and sensual, its movements languid under the falling water.

Raphael knew he should fire. It was right there, so close. All he had to do was shoot and he could get paid and get out of this place. Forget he'd ever laid eyes on—

But then it was before him. Fully illuminated, soaking wet. Streams of water kissed its form, highlighting the play of muscles across its abdomen and shoulders. The rain slithered down, down, into the sharp V of its hips, as if painting a trail to its groin. And its face—a heavy jaw with full lips, a broad nose and shining eyes.

Raphael's gaze stuck fast on the creature's mouth. It was the kind of mouth that bowed perfectly, the kind that made you want to brush your thumb across it and *push* until it opened for you.

His fear was momentarily abated as an entirely different kind of shiver ran down his spine.

"Are you the one they've sent to appease me?" the creature asked.

"I—I—" He hadn't expected it to speak. The grip on his gun loosened.

With steady strides, it came closer, its tail swishing back and forth behind it. It stopped right before it reached him, and lightly pushed the barrel of the shotgun away. "You don't need this," it assured him.

Its voice was dark and rich. A perfect gravel that rumbled through Raphael and went straight to his belly, coiling there like a spring.

"Last time they sent me a scrawny thing," it said, reaching out to lay its fingertips on Raphael's jaw. "They've done much better this time." It gazed at him intensely, not just with desire, but with feeling. It seemed to be looking into his mind, trying to understand him, to connect with him.

Raphael was lost in the gaze. "Who are you?" he breathed. "*What* are you?" He couldn't deny he felt small next to this thing, and he'd never felt small before in his life. Its hand was so close to his throat, and all it had to do was shift and *squeeze* and there would be nothing Raphael could do to save himself.

He'd never felt anything like that before, never felt like anyone could just do what they wanted with him. His pulse quickened.

"Do I excite you?" it asked, grasping his jaw tightly.

"Yes," he admitted. The coil in his belly had shifted to his groin, tightening, warming.

"Good." It smiled at him, soft and fond. But there was a slight smirk to it—an edge that promised dominance and passion. "I am Castor, god of the elder woods. Every year I require a tribute." It—no, *he*—leaned in close, bringing their mouths within a breath of one another. "That appears to be you, boy."

"I've been sent to kill you," Raphael said. The god was so close, he could smell him. Musky, spicy. The scent made Raphael's mouth water.

"Oh, is that so?" The god huffed an airy laugh, as though he knew Raphael had been tricked into coming.

Those damn hicks at the bar must have pulled this con before.

Ten grand for its hide, they'd said. How had he fallen for such bullshit?

He wanted to be angry. Wanted to spit in Castor's face and go back and give every last one of those bastards a whooping. Wanted to... wanted to...

Those lips were so close. Inviting. They were prettier than a man's lips had the right to be—god or otherwise. Raphael's tongue flicked out, almost of his own accord, wetting his own mouth but falling just short of touching Castor's.

I want... Raphael's brain stuttered. He could feel his pulse between his legs, filling his cock. *I want...*

Castor smiled. "You want to go to your knees for me, don't you?"

Raphael's dick twitched in his jeans. "Yes." He wanted that and more.

With a rumble of approval, Castor closed the distance between them, pressing close to Raphael's body, encircling him, towering over him. As Castor's lips captured his, he felt the god's erection press into his belly and he moaned. The line of it was hard and long against him.

The god's sinfully beautiful mouth kissed just as it should—deeply, languorously. Castor wasn't looking for a quick, dirty fuck. He wanted to revel in his tribute.

What were gods supposed to taste like? Were they supposed to taste the way pine needles smelled—fresh and green and delicious?

How was a god's body supposed to feel against a human's? All taut fire and rock-hard plains?

Raphael may have accepted his role as tribute, but he wasn't going to remain passive. As he moaned into Castor's mouth, he reached out for the god's ass, cupping it and drawing him forward to grind against him. They were both fully hard now, and Raphael was straining in his jeans, needing a hand on him, a mouth—something, anything. He just wanted his skin pressed up against Castor's.

As if reading his mind, the god pulled away, his tail flicking in an amused sort of way. "Aren't we eager?" he said, swiftly undoing Raphael's belt and yanking it free. "Give me your hands," he commanded.

Unsure, Raphael did as he was told. Castor took both of his wrists in one of his massive hands and pushed them together, wrapping the leather around them several times before buckling it tight. Grinning, he lifted Raphael's newly bound hands above his head, pressing them to the wood of the doorway.

Where there had been only smooth board before, now there was a massive gold hook, created by whatever magic the god possessed. Castor threaded the hook through the leather, forcing Raphael to keep his hands high above his head.

The position made his muscles strain, and he arched his back ever so slightly. Now the cling of his t-shirt had an obscene quality to it, and he felt exposed in the most debauched way.

Castor ran his large hands over Raphael's ribs, rucking up his shirt in the process and exposing his dark, damp skin. "What a good boy you are," Castor said. His voice held a heady, zealous quality, as though he were barely restraining himself. His eyes—which were indeed yellow—were fully dilated, and his cock stood out heavy and almost night-black between the two men. Precome dripped from it onto the stoop, and Raphael bit back a groan. He wanted to touch Castor so badly it ached. Flexing his fingers, he tugged at his restraints.

"Please," he begged, not really knowing what for.

Castor wrapped his hands around Raphael's hips, pulling them flush to his and making the human's back arch even further. When Raphael let out a filthy groan, Castor matched it, ducking forward to kiss him again. This time the kiss was frantic and deep. Castor's tongue eagerly probed between Raphael's lips, and the human matched him stroke for stroke.

When Castor broke away, Raphael tried to chase him, but the god held him back and chuckled. Moving at a slow tease, the god sank back on his haunches, bringing his face level with his tribute's groin. Taking great care, he peeled Raphael's jeans away, leaving his aching cock exposed to the night air.

"Yes," Raphael gasped. "Please. *Please.*"

The god played his fingers up and down Raphael's shaft, giving him just enough to make him writhe. "Do you want my mouth, tribute?"

"Yes."

Castor's tongue—which was long and wide—licked out quickly, grazing over the splayed head of Raphael's cock.

Raphael squirmed, seeking out more of that damp, soft heat.

With and appreciative growl, Castor sank forward, taking Raphael's entire length down his throat in one go.

Raphael's cock pulsed in appreciation. The god's mouth was so wet, and his cheeks were sucked in tight around his shaft. He could feel the head of his cock pressing into Castor's soft palate and sinking further still.

Unable to control himself, Raphael bucked his hips, eliciting a moan of approval from the god.

Then Castor's right hand was on Raphael's hip, the left toying with his sack while that inhuman tongue wrapped around his length and pumped—jacking him inside Castor's mouth.

The sensations were intense—like no other blowjob Raphael had ever received. He'd had more than a few talented mouths below his belt, but nothing compared to the pure bliss that was Castor's lips and tongue and throat.

Castor watched him while he worked. His sharp, yellow eyes held Raphael's gaze, urging him on. Raphael's arms strained as he pulled against the leather, pushing his entire body forward, wanting *more more more*.

"God, please. Please. *Yes*," he murmured as he moved his hips, watching his shaft sink again and again between Castor's stretched lips.

He was so close. Everything tingled—his balls, the base of his cock, his thighs. The coil in his belly tightened. Pressure built behind his abs. His mind went fuzzy with pleasure, and all he could focus on was chasing that wet heat to release.

Castor's fingers shifted from his sack, across his perineum to the soft pucker of his ass and he was gone. The light flick there sent Raphael soaring, eager to have the god anywhere and everywhere. Whatever Castor wanted, he could have. It was his, every inch of Raphael belonged to him.

One more hefty suck on his cock and Raphael was coming. The coil sprang free, sending blinding, intense pleasure through his groin and belly and limbs. Hot ropes of semen shot into Castor's mouth and he took them hungrily, swallowing down all Raphael had to give him.

The god hummed his appreciation, stroking Raphael's abs while he released, licking him through his aftershocks.

Still shuddering in ecstasy, Raphael gasped when Castor finally let him go, pulling off his spent cock with an obscene slurp. He now hung limply by his wrists, breath coming high and fast. His legs no longer wanted to support him, but he forced himself to remain standing.

Castor wiped his mouth on the back of his hand before laying a light kiss on Raphael's tingling lips. "Thank you for your tribute of seed," he whispered. "It is done, you did well."

"Wh-what?" Raphael asked, wincing as Castor released his hands.

"It is done. You have given your tribute." He massaged Raphael's arms, taking the human's weight and gently lowering him to the stoop.

A moment passed before Raphael could fully process what he was saying. Of course. Castor was a forest god—it was all about seed.

Castor sat behind him in the doorway, cradling him between his legs, supporting him against his chest. The god's erection was still hard against his back. "Will you go now?" Raphael asked.

"Do you wish for me to go?"

"No. I want—want to give you more. More tribute."

Castor growled into his ear, wrapping his arms around Raphael's chest and clutching him tightly. "Mmm. I would like that."

The rain had let up. It was little more than a sprinkle now, but the night was still a thick blanket over the forest. Everything was still quiet. "Should we go inside?" he asked.

Castor moved a hand beneath Raphael, cupping his ass and lifting him so that his pucker rubbed against Castor's thick cock. "I would rather have you here," he murmured against his ear.

Raphael caught sight of his forgotten shotgun and chuckled to himself. Only hours earlier he'd been determined to kill whatever was out here. Now he couldn't wait to have Castor ravage him. "Yes. Please," he begged again, grinning wickedly to himself as he was manhandled into position. Castor offered Raphael his fingers, and he sucked on them, slicking them as well as he could. "You won't have to go looking for tribute anymore." He gasped as Castor began prepping him. "I'll give you everything you need."

One finger. Then a second. "You'll stay with me?"

"I'm a hunter, I belong in the woods." A third finger. Raphael thrust himself back against the intrusion, ready to have the god buried deep inside.

Castor huffed a laugh against his ear. "You belong with me. The townspeople did well this year."

"Yes," Raphael agreed as Castor removed his fingers, leaving him momentarily empty. He let out another needy mewl as the head of Castor's cock pressed against his entrance. "Remind me to thank them."

Castor's mouth came down on the crook of Raphael's neck, biting hard as he slid himself home. Raphael let out a sudden cry of desire, and the forest was quiet no more.

The Road to Tartarus

By Gio Lassater

It had been ages since I had set foot within the temple of Zeus, but I still felt a part of it. I counted off the twenty-five steps from the ground to the main temple floor. My hand still felt the power of the mightiest of the gods when I pushed open the massive bronze doors. The scent of incense and blood filled my nostrils the way it always had.

I was home.

All the worshippers and aid seekers had gone home many hours ago. However, a straggler here and there offered up some form of sacrifice to the king of the gods. Whispered prayers fluttered from pillar to pillar, alighting on my ears like a soft butterfly that was as quickly gone.

Ignoring it all, I didn't stop walking until I stood before the immense statue of Zeus that took up the entire eastern wall of the temple. I spotted the worn stone where I had spent so many hours on my knees in service to my god.

"You have been away far too long."

I could not stop the smile from lips. "Tityrus, I thought he would have released you by now."

67

The old man chuckled when I turned to him. I took his hands in mine, kissing them in turn, and then kneeled before him. He placed his hands on top of my head, leaned down to kiss my forehead, and then pulled me to my feet.

"Let me look at you, Balius." He held me at arm's length, his eyes roving over every inch of my body. "You have been on the road far too long. I see it in the dust on your feet and the lean look of you. Zeus will not be pleased to see his favorite in such a state."

I waved away his concern. "I'm sure he has more important things to worry about besides a few pounds of fat lost." I hugged him.

"Your old room is still available," Tityrus said. He ushered me to a hidden door set within an alcove along the northern wall of the temple.

"I doubt I'll be staying that long," I said. I heard the sadness in my voice, and saw it reflected on the wizened face of my former master.

He nodded. "I feared as much. Your visitor arrived some time ago. He is waiting in the main dining hall."

"How long ago?" I asked.

"A few hours. Not long enough to get upset...yet."

"I remember the way," I said. "You go rest. I'll let you know if I need anything, and I promise to see you before I leave."

Tityrus shuffled off to his room. Watching him go, I realized how much I had missed him and my home in the temple. The desire to stay was overwhelming, but I pushed it away. There was no way I could.

When I reached the open doorway to the main dining hall, I stopped just inside and fell to my knees again. While I couldn't see the one I had come to meet, I knew that he saw me. To not show him deference would be courting disaster.

"And so you've come. At last." I could sense the beginnings of his irritation.

"I beg forgiveness for not arriving sooner. There was a storm."

"Damn Poseidon and his fickle nature anyway. Come in here."

I moved quickly to the far end of the room and stopped in front of the fire. My host stepped from the shadows of the corner. I had forgotten how imposing he was. Standing over seven feet tall, his body was covered in muscle that could inspire any sculptor. The white hair on his head flowed over his shoulders and accentuated the short facial hair hugging his face. A simple loincloth covered his groin. His slight smile and lightning-blue eyes melted my heart, and I hurried to take his outstretched hand.

He pulled me to him, bruising my lips with a kiss while his beard tickled my nose and cheeks. His free hand snaked beneath the hem of my peplos and cupped my ass.

"You've grown scrawny, Balius."

"And you're still as insatiable as ever, my lord Zeus."

His hand moved from my ass to the stony hardness of my cock. "You are one to speak, whelp."

We shared a laugh and another kiss.

"I missed you," he said. I could hear the sincerity in his words.

"And I you, lord Zeus."

"Enough of that," he admonished. "We have no need of formalities between us."

"Of course." I refilled his wine and poured some for myself. Before I could pull up a chair, he dragged me down onto his lap in a large wooden throne that materialized beneath us.

"I wish we had more time, but I have an important mission for you," he said.

Positioning myself so I straddling his lap while facing him, I reached beneath my peplos and pulled aside his loincloth, rubbing his massive erection along my cock, balls, and ass.

"Is it really so important?" I asked.

He took a large drink from his cup. "I'm afraid so. We shall have to become reacquainted at another time. Sadly. However, while we talk, you're welcome to stay where you are."

I kissed him and continued moving myself back and forth over his exposed cock. "What can I do for you, my lord?"

69

"I need you to travel to the underworld and negotiate for the return of Skylla," Zeus said.

"Isn't she one of Poseidon's horses? No wonder he's so angry," I said. "What happened?"

Zeus finished off the last of his wine, which I quickly replenished. "Damn them both! Poseidon helped some sailor that Hades had set his sights on. Because of that, Hades stole Skylla and is refusing to return her. Now they're both bickering back and forth, and of course, it falls to me to do something about it."

"Do you think Hades will release the horse to me?" I asked.

"I expect you to persuade him," Zeus said with a smile and wink. "I'll be damned if you haven't almost persuaded me to take you now, regardless of what I said."

When he reached under me, I sat up, fully expecting him to press his cock into me. I groaned when he lifted me up, kissed me, and then set me on the ground.

"Later. I promise," he said. "Now, I need you to leave. I have made arrangements with Charon to get you across Styx without paying the toll. I doubt Hades will be happy to see you, but I know you can persuade him."

"And if I can't?"

"Return here and send a message through Tityrus. I have to help Ares with a bit of nasty business, but if I have to pay Hades a visit, he will not relish the experience." He finished off the wine and tossed the cup aside. It disappeared before hitting the floor.

"I won't fail you," I promised.

He smiled and pulled me to him, ensuring his throbbing cock rubbed against my stomach through our clothing. "Either way, when we are finished, I will come and fulfill every desire you have. Twice."

†††

Before sending me on my way, Zeus used his power to reshape my body and make me more appealing to Hades. While Zeus preferred me to appear more lithe and willowy, he knew Hades would like me to have slight musculature and short brown hair. My cock he left as it was—long and curved slightly upward.

It took years before I became used to Zeus remolding me. My body never felt like my own, but knowing that it was pleasing to him was all that mattered. While I grew up in the temple with the express purpose of serving the king of the gods, knowing that I was favored by him above anyone else made life complete.

My pleasant thoughts and fantasies of Zeus were interrupted by the shouts of sailors. We had been at sea for a few hours on our journey to Taenarum. Poseidon had apparently been told of my mission because the strong wind at our back bore us along at a rapid clip. Looking over the railing I could see hippokampai moving beneath us. The sea god wanted Skylla returned quickly.

By the end of the day we pulled into a cove at the southern tip of the Peleponnese. The captain offered to send a small force of his men with me, but only I would be able to enter the underworld without dying. I thanked him and bestowed Zeus's blessing upon him before disembarking.

Finding Orpheus's cave took no time at all. Since very few went willingly into Hades' realm, there was no need to block the cave's entrance or hide knowledge of its existence.

The path through the cave was steep, rocky, and treacherous. Several times I lost my footing and feared I would dash my head on a huge boulder. Thankfully, once I had traveled for what felt like a couple hours, the path smoothed out. Only great stone stalactites hindered me, and those only occasionally. The darkness I dispelled with a torch.

Soon I heard water dripping from the ceiling obscured by dark mist far above me, and a soft, shushed whispering slowly built into moans intermixed with cries. A small rock bounced from the toe of my sandal and splashed into the water a few feet away.

I had arrived at the River Styx. Its grey waters splashed against skulls and bones littered along the black sand and rocks of the embankment. Occasionally a misshapen corpse would break the surface of the river before being pulled back under by unseen forces. I had subconsciously noticed a smell of death and decay once entering the underworld, but it became even more pronounced when I stopped at the river's edge.

"I was told to expect you." Charon emerged from the shadows, pointing his skeletal hand at a barge tethered to the left of the path. "Get in."

He said nothing else the entire time it took us to cross the river. Staying near the center of the barge, I kept my feet propped on the bench before me. While Zeus protected me and could retrieve me if necessary, I had no desire to let Styx drain my life away. One drop was all it would take.

Once we landed on the far bank, I stepped onto the spongy ground of Tartarus. I could feel the misery and longing of all the lost souls spread out before me. They moved at the edges of the light cast by my torch. My legs felt like they turned to stone, and my blood to ice. If Zeus hadn't sent me on this errand, I would turn around and leave.

"You will find my master is not welcoming of guests," Charon said. He stood directly behind me, and his presence sent chills down my spine.

"I have my mission. Thank you for your help." Without looking back, I strode forward, forgetting about the ferryman. My sights were set on Hades. He might not welcome me, but he could not so easily dismiss the envoy of his king.

† † †

I don't know what I expected the throne room for the ruler of the underworld to look like, but what stretched before me wasn't it. The unseen ceiling overhead was supported by massive columns of flesh that dripped with blood and writhed in apparent agony. The floor looked like black ice, slick and shiny while sucking light from the room. People attached to the walls by rusted hooks burned in place of torches, their screams and moans adding to the foreboding nature of the entire place.

A throne of skulls and bones materialized on the far side of the long room. I heard the sound of a mighty wind overhead, and a massive bat dropped down. Just before hitting the throne, the creature dissolved into mist, and Hades alighted on the floor. The vapor swirled around him and coalesced into an indigo exomis open across the right side of his chest. He sat upon the throne and casually rested one of his sculpted legs over the side.

I attempted to focus on his face, not what he truly wanted me to look at with the way he sat. Piercing grey-blue eyes set in a long slender face framed by a full brown beard looked upon me with disdain. Long hair rested upon his shoulder, and he brushed it aside. Upon reaching a respectful distance, I got on my knees and bowed to him. He waited longer than was customary or polite before acknowledging me.

"So, you are Zeus's whore, who he sends on behalf of the sniveling Poseidon." The tone of Hades' voice intended to give nothing but insult, but I chose to ignore it. He was baiting me, and there was no reason for me to take it.

"Lord Hades, my name is Bakus. I represent our king, Zeus. He sends his greetings and regrets that he could not be present himself." To show him that he wasn't in charge, I stood up and looked him in the eye. He stiffened but chose to say nothing about the affront. "I am pleased to make your acquaintance."

"I'm not giving Poseidon back the horse," Hades said. "He robbed me of something he knew I wanted. Skylla is my recompense."

A sigh died on my lips. I expected petulance, but the childish stubbornness that accompanied it—well, no, I expected that too. It's pretty much indicative of dealing with one of the spoiled gods, especially in their own domains.

"Lord Hades, I understand your—"

"You understand nothing!" The words echoed throughout the room for so long that I started to wonder if he wasn't using his power to do it. He shifted on the throne, exposing himself more, and stared down at me. Most likely as a tactic to intimidate me, he and the throne doubled in size in the blink of an eye.

Zeus did that all the time, and it no longer impressed me.

"You're correct. I'm sorry. I do not understand. Will you please help to?"

He wasn't expecting that.

"Croesus was to be my consort," Hades said.

"Croesus, is he the sailor Poseidon rescued?"

"Stole," Hades shouted. "He knew I had been looking after the man for some time. I made no attempts to hide my affections or intentions. I had presented myself to Croesus many times, wooing him and winning him over. The Fates told me he would soon journey to the Elysian Fields, and I hoped to bring him into my home, my bed.

"When Croesus's ship travelled too close to Charybdis the rest of his crew died, but Poseidon lifted him out of the water and set him on the land several miles away." Hades slammed his fist on the throne. "He defied the Fates, and he did it to spite me. Now Croesus is outside my grasp, and there is nothing I can do about it. So, yes, I took his damned horse. He robbed me. I robbed him."

"What do you want in exchange for Skylla?"

He laughed. "I want nothing. Well, nothing tangible anyway. Knowing that Poseidon is angry and seething is my reward. He constantly oversteps his bounds just because his waters cover so much of creation. Well, now he knows that his actions have consequences."

"You could still have Croesus," I said.

"I tried that with Persephone," Hades said with a sigh. "Her damned mother had to get involved, and now I have to deal with a sulking woman for four months out of the year. I have no desire to go through that with Croesus."

"He might come willingly."

"It is out of the question. Skylla will remain mine. You may leave. Now."

The people affixed to the walls burned brighter and screamed louder with the proclamation. Grey fog slowly swirled up from the base of Hades' throne. He may have intended for the meeting to end, but I didn't.

I stalked toward the throne and stopped with my hands on either of Hades' legs. He must have been very surprised by my actions because he shrank down to human size and stared intently at me. Shifting uncomfortably he opened his mouth to speak, but I cut him off.

"Lord Hades, please, let's not be hasty." I slid my hands up his legs, feeling the contours and strength of his muscles. Stopping at his thighs I moved my thumbs in small, slow circles, occasionally and seemingly unintentionally making contact with his expanding erection.

"Zeus regrets that Poseidon has acted the way he has. He wants peace within the family, and I'm here to make sure that happens." Leaning forward, I cocked my head to the side and smiled slightly. My tongue ran slowly over my lips. "Lord Hades, surely there is...something I can do in order to persuade you to continue the negotiations."

For the first time I realized that his skin was a smoky color that reminded me of the mist he used for show and effect. His exposed nipple was hard, and when he noticed me looking at it, he flexed the muscles of his chest. His exomis disappeared, leaving him completely nude before me.

"There are some things." He reached out and put his hand on the back of my head. His other hand wrapped around the base of his ample cock, pushing it down from where it rested against the rippling muscles of his abdomen. With little pressure, he brought my head down to marry my lips to the head of his cock.

My smile disappeared when Hades suddenly stopped me. I looked up at him, and his eyes burned with something that truly frightened me.

"Did you honestly think that it was going to be that simple?" Hades asked. "You thought you could just come into my realm, fuck me, and leave with my just recompense?" He laughed. "Stupid human."

"Lord Hades, I—"

"Spare me your hollow words." He waved his hand, and I found myself propelled away from him. Suspended above the floor, my arms and legs outstretched and immobile, he stalked toward me. "If this is how Zeus wants to handle the situation, fine. But, we're going to do it on my terms."

"You're not allowed to kill me." I was truly afraid of him at that moment. The look in his eyes was hungry and hateful.

"Oh, I wouldn't dream of it." He stopped in front of me and ran his hand from my chest, down my stomach, and then grasped my cock. Tugging on it, he brought me to full erection. His eyes never left mine. "I'm going to return Skylla to you. You'll walk out of here with her in tow. Let Poseidon have his damnable horse. I'll find another toy to satiate my desires.

"First, however, I'm going to enjoy you. I'm going to enjoy your screams, the sounds of your flesh being punished, the delicious melody of you begging me for mercy. And you have Zeus to thank for it all." Hades released his hold on me and snapped his fingers.

I suddenly found myself lying across a stone bench with my wrists shackled at the front and my bent legs pulled to the sides and shackled to great weights I could not lift. Feeling heat at my exposed ass, I looked over my shoulder...and wished I hadn't.

From the mist-shrouded darkness, a hulking beast appeared. At once I was reminded of King Minos' Minotaur. Stocky legs ending in hooves supported a massive torso riddled with more muscle than I had ever seen before. The great beast was covered with thick hair, and its powerful arms and hands were capped off with nightmare claws. Enormous bat wings protruding from its back kicked up a hurricane wind. The bellow from its great bull mouth sent shivers racing through me.

The creature was preceded by an already dripping cock that brought a scream to my throat. Its bulbous mushroom head, leaking copious amounts of precome, was engorged and purple. Low-hanging balls held enough come to fill me to capacity three times over.

I turned my head back, intent on begging Hades for mercy like he wanted me to, but my words were crushed by his cock being shoved into my mouth. All resistance died immediately as he forced the rigid tube of flesh past my lips and deep into my throat. My throat constantly constricted around his cock, eliciting moans from him and muted cries from me.

Finally, just when I thought I would pass out from lack of air, Hades pulled out, allowing me to cough and gasp. The creature behind me chose that moment to spread my ass open with his massive clawed hands, and a thick, broad tongue licked from my balls, over my quivering, expectant hole, and then back down.

Hades kneeled before me, slowly stroking himself. "The beast will be gentle, to start. I wouldn't want you passing out. But don't become complacent. I intend for you to earn Skylla's freedom."

"Zeus will have your head for this," I said through clenched teeth. The beast had stopped licking my hole and was rubbing its massive cock head in circles over the area.

Leaning forward, Hades slapped my face with his cock, leaving behind a saliva-coated stinging sensation. "You're just another mortal. Zeus has had dozens. He'll have countless more. He won't lose sleep over an ass stretched beyond reasoning. The sooner you realize that, the better off you'll be."

His erection in my mouth again stifled further conversation. I looked up just as he nodded at the beast. The hard flesh stopped moving in circles and began pressing into me. My breathing became my only focus as I willed myself to relax, open up, and allow the creature to enter me as easily as possible. It had obviously been bred for sexual torture, and I had no doubt it would fulfill Hades' every expectation.

My breath caught when the beast pressed forward. Hades thrust farther into my throat at the same time. My hole widened, and the cock continued inward. Just when I thought I would lose consciousness, the head was inside me. Spasms of pleasure and pain coursed through my body.

Hades picked up his pace, fucking my throat faster and faster until I saw his balls draw upward. Wave after wave of his hot come flooded my throat until he pulled back, washing my tongue. Still intent on remaining in charge—even though that possibility had long since fled—I swallowed everything he had to give me. I licked my lips and the remaining drop from the head of his cock when he pulled out.

Hades rubbed his slowly softening member on my lips and cheek, smearing them with saliva and the remnants of his godly seed. "Now the real fun begins."

I took a deep breath at the exact moment Hades stepped back. The creature pushed forward, filling me more than Zeus had ever imagined doing. Once I had even taken Zeus and Ares at the same time, but even that did not compare to the bull-demon.

Maintaining eye contact, Hades backed toward his throne and fell into it. Defiantly I began pressing backward, impaling myself more with the pulsating cock stretching me beyond imagining. Hades smirked and snapped his fingers. I screamed when the bull-demon lunged forward.

"You'll want to take your time," Hades said.

"Tell it to fuck me," I said, filling my voice with as much command and authority as I could. "Command your creature to fuck me like it's never fucked anything before."

"Truly?"

I slammed myself backward, gasping but refusing to scream. "Tell it to fuck me!"

"Very well. Beast, you heard the mortal. Destroy him."

The hulking creature snorted once and then thrust all the way inside me. Against my own will, I screamed and my vision turned to blackness. Breathing was the farthest thing from my mind. The rough stone bench tore at the flesh of my abdomen where the bull-demon's cock distended it from the inside.

Over and over the creature withdrew and pounded into me. My body was drenched in sweat and blood from the beast's claws tearing into the flesh of my back. Just when I thought I could take no more, the attack stopped. The manacles at my wrists and ankles disappeared. The beast lifted me from the bench, turned me around with its cock still buried deep in the battered recesses of my guts and began thrusting upward into me.

Grabbing onto its horns, I stared into the creature's eyes as it possessed me. The deep blackness of the eyes was empty of all feeling. The beast was fulfilling its role, fulfilling my wishes, fulfilling Hades' commands. I lost myself in the rhythm of the great cock pressing into me. Looking down I marveled when I saw the head constantly bulging outward against the flesh and muscle Zeus had so recently reshaped.

Without realizing it was happening, I gasped when come erupted from me. It painted the massive chest of the bull-demon, matting into the coarse hair. Come dripped from the creature's chin, and it licked its lips, savoring the taste. My orgasm went on and on, long after my balls had emptied themselves, the rush of emotion and release still lingered. Now I was ready to pass out from sheer ecstasy.

My eyes flew open when the creature grunted and pressed itself completely inside me. I could feel the forceful geyser its cock had become as spray after gigantic spray of come filled me. Quickly it became too much to contain, and the torrent flooded from my distended hole, bathing the creature in the fruits of its labors.

When the tide ceased, the creature laid me gently on my back on the bench. It withdrew its still erect cock from me, leaving me to feel empty even as more of its seed flowed from me and onto the floor.

Hearing footsteps, I leaned my head back and watched Hades approach me upside down.

He was stroking his once-again-erect cock, and just as he stopped, towering above me, he erupted. A fresh load of his come bathed my face and chest. Before he had finished, the bull-demon leaned down to clean me off with its tongue.

"You have earned your prize. Was it worth it?"

I smiled. "I got what I wanted, so yes."

Hades scowled. His arm turned to smoke and trailed over my sweat-slick body, flowing into my still gaping hole. The mist filled me and coalesced. I came again just from the sensation of being full. The creature cleaned me off.

"I could rip you inside out and toss your carcass to the wretched souls of Tartarus," Hades hissed.

"You cannot kill me," I reminded him. "Zeus would fuck you with your own cock and then force you to eat it—while I watched and laughed."

Hades jerked his hand back, eliciting a sound between a moan and a scream from me. "Take Skylla and get out of my realm. Tell Zeus you are to never return."

"I go where Zeus pleases." I rolled onto my feet from the bench, steadying myself on the beast's arm. "Zeus will be sending for one of these. I absolutely have to experience that again."

Hades scowled and waved his hands. My laughter echoed from the walls of his throne room, but died in the sounds of surf and sea birds. Standing up, I trudged along the beach toward the waiting ship. In the distance I saw a magnificent horse staring back at me. It whinnied before a tidal wave washed over it, dragging it into the welcome clutches of Poseidon.

The Birthday Gift
By Arabella

Manny sipped his wine and tried to ignore the throbbing music coming from the club downstairs. Stroking his cat's tail, he smiled at his roommate, Kim.

"So, how many people did you invite to this do?" he asked.

Kim licked his lips. "Only twenty or thirty. Not a lot. Come on. You know you'll have fun. It's your birthday."

"Twenty or thirty or fifty, maybe? The club is packed!"

"I wanted everyone to be here to help you ring in the big four-oh. You've been such a prude thinking that you're losing your hair and putting on love handles."

Kim sidled up next to Manny, slid his arm around his waist, and squeezed the bit of flesh barely peeking over his jeans. He pressed warm lips against Manny's neck and followed his collar line with a row of nibbles.

"I think you're sexy, even if you don't and I know a way to loosen you up. Make you forget all those old age nerves," Kim whispered and reached between Manny's legs and gave a gentle squeeze.

Manny grabbed Kim's face and kissed him hard, slipping his tongue into his mouth. A hot surge pulsed between Manny's legs. He pulled his lips away but kept his fingers laced in Kim's hair. He loved Kim more than he'd ever loved anyone, but turning forty was not a milestone he wanted to face, not even in the midst of a group of friends and family helping him forget.

"I'd rather save that for when we have time alone," he said. "I guess we should join the party."

Kim's warm hand slid through what remained of his receding hairline and massaged the nape of his neck.

"You'll love it. I bought you the perfect gift. Something to take your mind off growing older."

Manny frowned. "Keep rubbing it in. I thought you said this was to help me forget, so quit mentioning it every two seconds."

"Fine." Kim tugged on his arm. "Let's go down."

They descended into the club on the lower level of the old brownstone. Most weeknights it was silent, but the weekends typically made up for it. Tonight was a Tuesday though. The neighbors weren't going to be happy if the party lasted long. Lights flashed frantically, the beat of pop music vibrated through every surface, and as the two men entered the room, the crowd shouted and whooped.

Streamers and poppers sailed through the air which was already atomized with alcohol. A pile of gifts flooded a table shoved into a corner. The rest of the furniture was pushed against every available wall except for a single round table placed directly in the center of the room.

On it rested a skull and forty candles of every shape, size, and color Manny could imagine. The flames flickered with each pulse of the music.

"Congratulations!" A young man with spiked hair plunged his hand into Manny's.

"Thanks, Rod," he yelled.

Someone patted his shoulder, and he turned to face a woman with gray hair, permed like his grandmother always wore. Manny wrapped an arm around her shoulders.

"Gwendolyn! How lovely to see you!"

"What? I can't hear you," Gwen shouted.

This wasn't going to be much fun if he couldn't talk to anyone. He scanned the room for Kim and waved him over.

"Can we turn down the music, please?"

Kim pursed his lips together but nodded and disappeared behind the bar at the far end of the room. Moments later the music dimmed noticeably.

Everyone uttered a communal sigh of relief and then broke into laughter.

Manny relaxed into a chair near the center table and crossed his legs to conceal the enlarged member he still sported. Damn Kim anyway for getting him all worked up.

One of the candles on the table sputtered and went out with a hiss, wax ran in a thin stream down the side and pooled on the laminate into a black shimmering blob.

Gwen pulled up a chair and sat beside him, crossing her legs and leaning close. She put a hand on his knee and squeezed.

"You know I used to be a man, right? I understand the problem."

Manny stared. In all the years he'd known Gwen, Gwen had been an older woman, long grey hair, thin frame, beautiful thin jawline, glowing skin.

"You were … I'm sorry, I'm shocked. I shouldn't be. You've just always been … a woman."

Gwen ran her hand up his groin. He flinched.

"I'm just kidding you honey. Did it help?"

"You wicked woman. Curse you!" Manny exclaimed.

A breeze brushed the hair on his arm. Another flame sputtered and blew out. Red wax pooled in a perfect disc under a two inch candle.

"What is the deal with the candles? Only one at a time goes out." He picked up a burning candle and relit the other two.

They both flickered for a moment and then sizzled out again. A third candle choked as well, melting into another red puddle.

Hands grasped his shoulders and squeezed. Lips, warm and soft, planted on his neck and crawled up to behind his ear. His dick pulsed again.

"Damn you, Kim. Stop or I'll never get through this evening."

Gwen laughed and vacated her seat.

Kim slid into it and leaned close, handing Manny a glass of wine. "Well, we could go in the back and have a quickie. Relieve that frustration."

Manny kissed Kim, gently at first, and ran a hand through his hair. Then kissed him again, full on, pulling his tongue into his mouth. The adrenaline of the moment took over as he sucked hard on Kim's tongue, firm in his mouth. His breathing quickened, his dick twinged with expectation.

"You two should get a room!" Rod called from behind them. "Come on. This is a party. Let's get the balls rolling boys."

Manny released his kiss and pulled his head up. His lips tingled with warmth, full of the heat of the moment.

Kim laughed, a full on raucous "Ha, ha, ha!" from the pit of his stomach and stood up, brushing against Manny's arm as he did so, with his throbbing dick threatening to rip through his jeans.

Another candle flickered and went out leaving a pool of green wax dripping off the edge of the table.

Manny took a deep breath, the feel of Kim's erection not helping to quell his own excitement of things to come, and caught some of the wax on his finger. He rolled it into a sphere, soft and sensuous, and squeezed it gently between his thumb and finger. He sipped from his glass, the heady aroma of Chardonnay filling his nose, and then raised it high. "Well, if no one else is going to toast me, I'll toast myself. I just want to say thank you to everyone for coming and celebrating this auspicious day. Happy birthday to me!"

The room erupted into a cacophony of "Happy birthday!" and "Cheers!" and whoops and hollers. Glasses clinked and everyone shuffled near the table.

Several candles fizzled out, adding more drips and blobs of colored wax to the laminate surface.

"Anyone want to tell me what all these candles and this skull mean?" Manny asked. "Other than I'm turning forty and therefore I'm about to die of old age?" He laughed despite is apprehension about his age.

Kim returned with a present in his hand and gestured over the remaining flames in a broad motion. "It's all part of the ritual to help you see past this milestone in your life and into your future. The light of the candles is to give you hope that your future will be bright and the different colors all mean different things. Like orange is for happiness and success and blue is to help you find contentment."

He picked up a red candle, still burning, and let a drop of wax land in Manny's wine. "And red ... red is for sexual attraction."

A flush rose up Manny's face. Sweat beaded on his forehead.

Two men grabbed gifts from the table in the corner and brought them over.

Relieved by the distraction, Manny reached out and snuffed another candle with his fingertips and smiled. Dark blue wax dripped erratically, building up in a ragged column along the side.

"Open mine first," a bald man said. He held out a blue pyramidal package covered in swirls and stars.

Manny ripped it open, dropping the paper on the floor. An orange mass of rock appeared. It was heavy and had a plug.

"What's this?" he asked.

The man frowned. "A salt lamp. It releases negative ions which are good for your health. It gives you energy and keeps you from getting headaches when using your computer and other electronics. I can't believe you don't know what they are."

"Oh wow. That sounds amazing. Thank you." He set in on the floor under the table of candles wondering if he could return it. Foofoo mysticism, new age stuff wasn't his thing, even if it was remarkably phallic. Maybe he'd keep it just for that purpose and bring it out to set the mood.

The next package was handed to him, and he tore the newspaper wrapping.

"Ah. A mustache cup." He didn't have a mustache. No need to drink from what looked like a grown-up sippy cup. He smiled. No sense in stating the obvious. He placed it on the floor with the salt lamp.

He opened presents for the next few minutes acquiring a new tie, a box of chocolate truffles, and other assorted odd things. Then Kim sat down beside him and handed him the inconsequential box with a colossal red bow he'd been holding since the beginning.

"Wow, honey. What's this? Such a massive ribbon." He pulled off the lid, tucked it on the edge of the table, and opened tissue paper.

A small stuffed doll stared at him, burlap edges fraying wildly. Long metal pins, each with a different colored ball on the end, lay beside it.

"Um … a voodoo doll?" Manny scrunched up his face in confusion and peered at Kim.

Kim took the doll from the box and placed it on the table with the candles, accidentally extinguishing two white ones. "It's good luck. I promise. Voodoo dolls are meant to cast goodness and bring happiness, not all that sinister nonsense you see in the movies." He took the box from Manny as well, and pulled out the pin with the red ball on it.

"This one is for love, I think. You pin it straight through the middle of the doll like this." Kim stabbed the pin into the burlap heart.

Gwen shouted, "No!" but it was too late.

Manny felt queasy. His heart thumped wildly and he gasped for a breath of air.

Gwen pushed Kim away from the table and gestured madly. "What have you done? You can't just go jabbing pins in places like you do with your dick. There is a proper way. You have to learn the ritual."

Kim held up the blue pin. "I read all about it, Gwen. I know what I'm doing."

She tried to stop him by placing her hand over the doll. "No, Kim. Can't you see you hurt him?"

Kim frowned and tried to reach around her. "Gwen, I know what I'm doing. Really. Madam Toulouse showed me. If I do them in the right order it will all work out."

He managed to grab the doll from under Gwen's hand and held it up for everyone to see. "This one is for merging souls, like soul mates, forever. It goes in the side to show that two people are joined at the ribs, like Adam and Eve. And that's how I always want to be with Manny."

The party guests oohed and awed at the sentiment. Someone whistled in the back of the room. Another guest called out, "Kiss him!"

Kim leaned over, whispered into Manny's ear, and then kissed him again, gently this time. "I promise this will be the best things that's ever happened to us, honey. Trust me?" He stood up and stabbed the pin in the side of the doll.

Manny coughed and gasped for air. His stomach churned and with each cough vomit inched closer to his throat, threatening to spew. His chest felt heavy.

"I can't catch my breath," he said.

Gwen jerked the pin from the doll and turned to Kim. "What in God's name are you doing to him?"

The hand holding the doll moved just enough to catch the fraying edges in one of the candles flames. One leg caught fire and singed toward the crotch.

Manny jumped up from his chair, his breath returned as heat rose up his inner leg. His dick pushed against his pants, throbbing in the warmth.

The whole club went silent watching him spin around holding his pants.

He bumped into the table knocking candles everywhere.

Sparks caught wrapping paper on fire. The gifts went up in flames.

The bald guy's pants started burning, and three of the other guests threw him to the floor and rolled him around until the fire went out.

The skull rolled lopsided and landed next to Manny's foot. He bent over and picked it up, holding it in front of his pulsing groin. He hadn't wanted this party to begin with, but this was a little ridiculous.

Kim grabbed the doll from Gwen and blew out the flames. "What the hell? I didn't mean for any of this to happen. I was supposed to stick the pin in and Manny was supposed to fall hopelessly in love with me and want to spend eternity together!" He gripped the doll tightly in one hand.

Manny choked and began slapping his own chest trying to breath, again.

Kim released the doll. "Oh my gawd, I am so sorry." He stepped over to Manny and ran his hand through his hair gently. "Are you okay?"

Manny grabbed the doll from Kim's hand. "Where did you get this, and why on earth would you go to such …" He let the question die out as the reality of what Kim said took hold. "You did this because … you want me to …"

Kim nodded, a hopeful smile on his face.

Manny stared at the doll for a moment and then gazed into Kim's eyes. "I'm already hopelessly in love with you and want to spend the rest of my life with you, I just didn't know you felt the same way so I hadn't said anything. You didn't need a voodoo doll to make this happen."

Kim grinned and looked around the club. The burned gifts smoldered in the corner, candle wax littered the floor, and the party goers stood huddled together, a mixture of fear and awe on their faces.

"Well, it worked didn't it?"

Manny gawked for a moment. He was right. It had worked, just not in the way anyone thought it would.

"You know, Kim, love of my life, this is not the birthday I would have planned for myself, but you're voodoo magic will certainly make it the most memorable one I've ever had."

Manny grabbed Kim and planted a huge kiss on him, sinking his tongue deep into his mouth. He didn't let go until he couldn't breathe any more. Excitement pulsed through his whole body. His cock hardened against his pants.

The crowd cheered as loud as they had when the party first started.

Kim blushed but smiled. "Well let's get this cleaned up and start rocking this party the right way! Next time we see you all it will be for a wedding!"

He took the little doll from Manny, smoothed the stray fibers of burlap around the head, and kissed it gently. He found the singed box it came in on the floor beside the overturned table and picked it up. Placing the doll back in, he closed the lid and put it in his shirt pocket.

"No telling when I'll need it again, but it's safe for now, right next to my heart."

Everyone cheered again, including Manny this time.

The men embraced. Manny kissed Kim's neck and squeezed his balls gently until Kim moaned. Then he whispered in Kim's ear, "Just wait 'til I get you home tonight. Oh the things I will do to thank you for this birthday gift."

Kim leaned his forehead against Manny's. "Just wait until you see what else I can do with this voodoo doll. All of those things you don't like about turning the big four-oh, I can make them go away. You'll see what magic really is."

Gwen stood up behind the bar with a white box in hands, and called out, "Time for love making later. First we have to have cake and blow out the candles."

Everyone cheered and clinked glasses and restored the furniture to how it was before the accident, while Gwen removed a sheet cake from the box and arranged candles all over the top. She carried it to the center of the room and placed it on the table. The inscription read "Happy Birthday to the Handliest Manny!"

Kim frowned at it. "That's not what I told them to put. It's supposed to say Manliest Manny."

Gwen nudged him. "It is kind of funny though." A smile spread across her face.

Manny wrapped an arm around both of them and declared, "It's perfect. I love it! Let's get the singing over with." Kim's statement about what else the voodoo doll could do for him had him intrigued and wondering. Maybe he could have a full head of hair again and clear up those laugh lines around his eyes.

Gwen cleared her throat and sang a pitch, then directed the room with one hand. Everyone joined in singing Happy Birthday.

When they finished, Manny made his wish, leaned over, and blew on the candles until every last flame was extinguished. More cheering ensued as he cut the cake and handed out pieces.

The music started playing "Love You A Long Time", drowning out the voices in the room. Manny and Kim danced, arms encircling one another.

Manny leaned his head into Kim's shoulder and nibbled on his ear. Kim returned the gesture, and Manny's whole body tingled with excitement. "I can't wait 'til later. Let's go."

Kim smiled, looped his arm through Manny's, and led him up the stairs to their apartment. As they closed the door, he removed the box from his pocket and took out the doll. He rubbed his fingers along the sides of it gently, pressing just enough to flatten the edges.

A strange sensation rippled through Manny's stomach, tightening the muscles in every direction.

Kim laid the doll down on the back of a leather sofa in the middle of the room. He pulled Manny close and removed his shirt, warm fingers sliding up his skin, finding his nipples and squeezing softly.

Manny gawked at the sleek six-pack of toned abdominals he sported. Tingling jolts pulsed through him at Kim's touch. "How did you do that?"

Kim just smiled, leaned close, and took one of Manny's nipples in his lips. His tongue massaged the end gently.

Manny grabbed Kim's head, and ran his hands through Kim's hair. "If that was voodoo, do it again."

Kim moved to the other nipple, repeated the action, and then ran his tongue down Manny's chest, warm and sensuous. He kissed each toned abdominal.

Manny's cock swelled, hot and hard. He unzipped his pants and let them fall to the floor and then stepped out of them, kicking off his shoes. He removed his boxers and stood naked, his dick pulsating in rhythm to the music from downstairs.

He tugged at Kim's shirt, untucking it from his pants.

Kim pushed him away and began to unfasten the buttons slowly. "You have to wait. I'm not through with the charms." He grinned and picked up the voodoo doll again.

This time he used one of the long pins and teased strands of burlap from the top of the head.

The feeling of tiny pin pricks rippled across Manny's head. It wasn't uncomfortable, more like having something with menthol rubbed into his skin. He reached up and found a whole head full of hair, like he'd had in his twenties. "What the...? That doll is like the fountain of youth!"

Kim smiled and nodded. "I told you to just wait and see. And I'm not through yet." He removed his shirt, tucked the doll in the waist band of his pants, and pulled Manny close again. Running hands through his hair, he kissed him and moved him toward the sofa.

Manny undid the snap and zipper on Kim's jeans and ran his hand down the back side, caressing Kim's butt cheeks.

The doll slid into Kim's crotch. He retrieved it with one hand and ran the other along Manny's unyielding shaft, massaging the base with his fingers, before cupping his balls and pressing against the lip of skin behind them.

A moan slipped from Manny's throat as a wave of ecstasy surged up his spine and made him feel almost drunk. He leaned closer, grabbing Kim's hand and pressing it in to his g-spot.

Kim pulled away. This time he turned the doll over and ran one finger down its back and between the legs.

Manny screamed in delight. Stars exploded all around him.

Kim teased. "Did you like that? I can do it again…maybe." He removed his pants and underwear, losing his shoes in the pile of them. He pulled Manny to the sofa, laid him down, and kneeled over him, face-to-face. "Or I can do something you like even more."

Kim's body was warm against Manny's legs. It made his dick throb until it was rigid and hot. He couldn't wait any more.

Kim kissed the doll between the legs and placed it gently on the floor beside them.

Manny shouted with pure pleasure, as Kim's lips enveloped the head of his cock and sucked slowly and deliberately, his tongue massaging in a methodical circle around and around and around. Electric shocks soared through his body, rippling his newly formed abs, and tingling his scalp full of hair, until his vision went black, and he came like he hadn't done since he was in college. It was exhilarating.

He moaned. "That was the best fuck I think I've ever had," he said. "I don't know what that voodoo doll does, but we are keeping it in a safe place. We should even get one for you, too."

Kim was all smiles. He reached down and picked up the burlap doll. "I'm glad you like your birthday gift, my love! Are you ready for another round?"

Biters

By Gio Lassater

Going out at night is the worst. No streetlights or soft glow from the windows of houses lining the streets. Just the dim bulb of a flashlight lets me see.

I only go out at night when I have to, but that decision isn't always mine. Part of being with the community is doing what you're told, what you have to do in order to survive. We never know how long the food is going to last. The only way we stay strong, the only way we survive, is finding and storing as much food as possible.

I move quietly along the broken, pitted sidewalk on the north side of a once-busy street. The former shops I pass hold nothing of value or interest to me now. No one needs a computer without electricity or internet. What good would a new business suit be when my job is not getting killed?

A few paces ahead of me, Camden holds his fist up beside his head seconds before he stops and crouches down. I always feel better when he's on point. His hearing is better than anyone else's, and he has night vision that seems supernatural.

I kneel behind Cam and close my eyes, remembering to switch off the flashlight before I blind him. Still unable to hear anything, I consciously focus on my breathing and attempting to keep my adrenaline under control. The last thing we need is for me to lose it and get us killed out of sheer stupid terror.

Cam holds up one finger briefly before a second finger joins it. There are two creatures; I'm thankful there aren't more. We should be able to take care of them without a problem. Our destination is only a few blocks away, and I don't want to backtrack and go around. Not tonight.

I slip the flashlight into my jacket pocket and grab the knife at my hip. There's no sound as I pull the blade from its leather sheath. The hard handle and weight of the knife feels good in my hand. It gives me comfort. I can do this. I can do this.

Cam squeezes my hand, and then we move cautiously along the broken, pitted sidewalk. Now I hear what he heard minutes ago, and I'm thankful—again—that I have him with me. He keeps me alive. Sometimes I'm torn over whether that's a good thing or not. Tonight it is. When it's just the two of us on a mission, everything feels right. I know I can keep going.

Near the mouth of an alley so dark it might as well be in outer space, Cam stops and peeks around the corner. While I wouldn't be able to see anything, he can pick out the various bits of debris littering the narrow confines between one building and the next. He leans out farther, pauses, then leans back and turns to me.

I move close, and he puts his mouth near my ear to whisper, "They're in there. I'm going to draw them out. Be ready."

We kiss for luck. We always do in these situations. It reminds us that we're alive and gives us a reason to keep going. We live because we don't want the other to be alone. We fight so hard because we don't want the other one to leave us. I have no delusions, though. Cam would survive without me, but the reverse isn't true.

He breaks the kiss and turns back toward the alley. Fishing a rock from his pocket, he tosses it into the narrow opening, and then tosses another one toward the street to our right. I press against the building, inching my way upward until I'm standing. My heart pounds. My lungs want to gulp as much air as they can, but I govern them. My bladder threatens me with embarrassment.

The stench of death and decay precedes a death-rattle-like moan. My stomach joins most of the rest of my body in rebellion. I quell it, and grip the knife tighter. I have to stay alive for Cam.

The first creature stumbles out. Cam threw a rock right before that, and it clatters down the street, drawing attention away from us. The second one comes right after. It sees Cam move to take out the first one and lunges at him. They go down in a heap of flesh and noise that has disastrous potential.

Pushing away from the wall, I run full-speed at my target. It stretches its hands out toward me, its fingers clutching the air repeatedly. With a slide-run step, it barrels forward, intent on nothing but a meal.

That single-mindedness works for me. At the last possible second, I duck and glide around the monstrosity's right side. By the time it reaches down to grab me, I'm behind it. The knife pierces the blackened flesh and jellied skull. Using its momentum, I pull the knife out while the twice-dead body falls to the ground.

There is no victory celebration. The only time I ever did that, one of them came up behind me. Cam put it down when its mouth is only inches from me. I didn't sleep for several days after that, and I never repeated that mistake.

Cam is on his knees beside his attacker. The fingers of its detached arm clench in the fabric of his shirt. He rips it away and throws it into the alley with a distant wet *squish*. He's not even breathing hard after the ordeal.

"It's over." The whispered words sound so stupid to me. It's *not* over. The only way it's going to be over is to die—hopefully in a way that prevents us from coming back as one of these things.

Cam stands up and leans back against me. I know he thinks it's a sign of weakness. I see it as him trusting me and letting me support him. My left arm wraps around him, and I rest my head on his shoulder. He takes a deep breath, holds it, and slowly lets it out.

"I'm fine. Let's go." He kisses me at an awkward angle and pulls away.

Cam picks up the pace. A block away he stops, and like before I don't hear anything. He only holds up one finger, and over a few seconds, he slowly lowers it. The zombie is moving away.

I see the silhouette of our destination against the darker night. I've been here once, but Cam comes often. On his last run, he stashed a few bags full of food because he had to retreat from a small horde. He baited them away, so they should have moved on. It's possible they came back, or others have taken their place, but our scouts didn't find any evidence of further infestation.

Cam stops in front of a broken window, and I bump into him because I'm paying more attention to the past than the present. I'll hear about that later, but for now, I chastise myself worse than he ever could.

He signals me to stay and wait. I start my pre-arranged count to twenty when he steps over the windowsill into the dangerous confines of the convenience store. Glass crunches under his feet. I look around to see if we've drawn a crowd, but we're alone.

My count hits twenty, and my heart is pounding. I hate fucking darkness! I hate being *alone* in the darkness. It's the worst. Now I'm going farther into the darkness.

I make slightly more noise stepping onto the glass than Cam did. There's only silence coming from farther inside. That means he's alone, and that he's most likely made it to his stash. A single low whistle alerts me to his return. I take one of the bags from him. Within seconds, we're back over the sill and on our way back to our base.

That was the plan, at least.

A bright light shines into my eyes, blinding me. Cam grunts behind me, and I hear a struggle. Our bags hit the ground simultaneously. Something hard hits me in the side of the head, and I land on my stomach. I see spots, but I push myself to my knees. A heavy boot in the center of my chest sends me onto my back. My head smacks against concrete and glass.

Someone sits on me, pinning my arms to the ground with his knees. The stink of his breath isn't as bad as zombie rot, but only barely. A face without definition hangs in the air above mine. He runs a hand along my cheek.

"We're taking the food. If you fuck with us, we'll take more." Cold metal presses against my throat. "Go back home and forget this happened. Understand?"

"Yeah." Let him think I'm giving in. In my mind, plans turn and form. He thinks he can do this and get away with it, but if his friend hurt Cam, I'll feed them both to zombies.

"Porter, you got your shit?" Ass-breath asks.

"Yeah. I think the fag is dead, though."

"Who gives a shit? Get the bag and let's go." He leans close to me. "Remember, piss off and forget about this."

He slaps my face, and then he's gone.

I ignore the pain in my face, chest, head, and back. Hell, my whole body is a giant miasma of agony and screaming nerves, but that doesn't matter. Ass-breath's friend said Cam was dead. I have to know.

The thought I might have to splatter his brains on the sidewalk knocks at the back of my mind, but I refuse to answer that door. He's not dead. He's not dead.

Oh, thank god, he's not dead.

"Ian." The words are a whisper torn from a throat lined with a cheese grater and sand paper. He said my name; he never says it when we're on a mission. He has some silly superstition because he thinks if he doesn't say my name outside of our base that I'll keep coming home. He'll never lose me. It's worked so far, so who am I to tell him he's wrong?

"I'm here, baby. Are you okay?" I kneel beside him and fish the flashlight from my pocket.

"Fuck, my eyes!" His hand flies in front of his face.

"Sorry. I need to see if you have any injuries." I shine the light along his body.

"Too many injuries to count."

"I mean of the fatal variety, so shut up. You're the eagle eye; I'm the physician. Let me be that for one goddam minute, will you?" My fear comes out as anger, but I don't apologize.

"Sorry," he says in my stead.

I just find scrapes and bruises. The worst is a piece of glass sticking into the back of his arm, but we have enough first aid supplies to cover everything.

"You'll live," I say.

"Shit. We need to move."

I help him to his feet. There's no need to ask what's going on. He's heard something, and we may not have much time before it gets to us. The thought that he didn't hear the thieves flits through my mind, but I'm more to blame than he is. They shouldn't have been able to sneak up on us. That's when I realize Cam's probably thinking the same thing, but he's not saying anything about it.

Both of our knives are gone. Those bastards took everything, leaving us defenseless. However, there's no time to worry about that. We take off, moving quicker than we normally would. With Cam on point, though, I feel safe and confident.

Not far from our base, Cam slows down and walks into the recessed entrance of a building we cleared out months ago and boarded up to use as a sanctuary, if needed.

"I'm going to hang back to make sure we're not being followed," he says. "We don't want them knowing where we live. Go a few blocks past and then circle around to the back entrance. I'll be home as soon as I can be."

"Be safe. I love you." I press our bodies together. It could be the last time I feel him, kiss him.

"Go on." He trails a hand along the spot he doesn't realize Ass-breath slapped earlier.

I leave him to cover my back, keeping my pace slow enough that I might be able to hear if he has to take on someone. My eyes scan what little of the area I can see. No telltale dark spots that could be wandering zombies. No assholes attacking from the shadows.

Home used to be an office building situated between a residential area and a nearby shopping complex. Both of them have provided resources, and we haven't had to go too far to get them. With all of the rooms in the building, it didn't take much to convert offices into bedrooms. Some of them even feel spacious.

Mandy is on sentry duty at the back door, and she lets me in. My body screams for rest and water. She gives me a look full of questions and doubts. Explanations will have to wait. I need water and to make sure Cam gets home safely. I run to the main entrance for a vigil I hold too frequently.

At the front, I stare through the slit we left in the metal door so we can stab monsters in the head. There's no light this close to the entrance. We reserve light for the interior rooms only when it's necessary.

"What happened?" Darren asks from his post at a nearby-barricaded window.

I explain the situation quickly, never taking my eyes away from my vigil. It's only been ten minutes since I left Cam, and it's driving me crazy. He can take care of himself, but that doesn't mean I'm not entitled to—

"There." I point at a shape moving through the darkness. It runs from one of our barriers to another. When we settled here, we set up various piles of debris at random intervals throughout the path leading to the front doors. It was an attempt to look as natural as piles of garbage could look in order to give ourselves cover and cut down on the number of zombies that can come at us at once. Some people also think it helps not to attract unwanted attention from other survivor groups that might decide to take us on.

Like Ass-breath and his friend.

Cam's whistle reaches my ears, and I help Darren to unbar the doors and let him in. We close the doors once he's inside, and I tell him to go to the infirmary. A fancy name for the room where we keep the first aid kit; where I pretend I'm still a doctor, not a monster slayer. I chuckle at the thought, and motion Cam onward when he turns to look at me.

The light in the infirmary reveals a horrific tableau. Cam looks like he dived into a swimming pool filled with blood and used his hands to brush away a few spots here and there. A coppery smell permeates the room, but I've smelled worse.

"Were we followed?" I ask.

"Yes. It was probably a scout, not one of our attackers. That's why they let us go." Cam pulls his shirt over his head and tosses it onto the floor. The *splorch* it makes echoes in my ears.

"Did you..."

"I had to, Ian. I didn't want to, but I had to." He falls into a chair and runs his hands through his hair. It makes him look like a gory greaser. "If they find us, they won't hesitate to try to take our stuff. Our people would get hurt. I don't want that."

"Neither do I." I pour a small amount of water into a metal tub with a hole rusted in the side and wet a scrap of cloth.

"I know you don't," Cam says. "I wasn't trying to say..." He sighs. "I know, baby. I'm sorry if you thought that's what I meant. We've seen some shit tonight."

"You more than me," I say.

"That's how I want it to be."

"I'm not helpless. I just don't like being out at night." I wipe blood from his face and rinse the cloth. "I hate that you've had to kill someone again."

"I know."

"That's what you say when you want me to shut up."

"I know." He grins, and it makes him look like a nightmare creature fresh from the kill.

I toss the cloth to him. "Clean up as best you can, and I'll check you over. We have to make sure there's no chance of infection."

"I'm fine. I promise."

"Humor me."

"Anything for you, love."

†††

Our bedroom is a mess of scattered weapons, discarded clothes, and a mattress scavenged from a nearby furniture store. Whomever this room belonged to before we commandeered it really liked motivational posters. We left them hanging on the stark white walls to remind ourselves of a different time. Not necessarily better, but different.

Weak sunlight filters into the room from a small window at the top of one wall. I have no idea why anyone would have put that there, but since the building didn't originally house offices, maybe it's a throwback to an earlier life. I close my eyes and will myself to relax, but my brain isn't having it.

I can't help but think about the man that Cam killed. How did he do it? What did he do with the body? Did he leave it somewhere for a zombie to find? They don't usually eat dead things. Maybe he left the person alive but wounded to the point he couldn't get back to his people. I shouldn't think about these things.

"Ian, go to sleep." Cam rolls over to snuggle up behind me. "I'm sorry I killed him, but I had no choice."

"I know."

"Hey, that's my line." He kisses the back of my neck. "I'm sorry you have to deal with this stuff."

"I've seen worse." I was a doctor in a large city. I've seen my fair share of truly horrible inhumanity.

"You deserve better than this."

I turn over to face him. "Do you think I'm weak?"

"I think you're the strongest person here. Well, with the exception of Bert, but that's only because he's a fucking psycho with no feelings." He runs his hand through my long hair, which is somehow shaggier than his is.

"I just have all these thoughts and doubts that run through my head. All the time, they're there, but they really come out when we go on runs." I roll onto my back so I don't have to look at those green eyes staring at me while I unburden myself. "You're so sure of yourself. You keep people alive, and nothing seems to faze you. I know it does, don't get me wrong, but you're so good at hiding it."

"That's not necessarily a good thing," he whispers. His hand glides over my chest, and he pulls me close. "We all do what we have to do, and we all freak the fuck out in our own way. If you could see inside my head, you'd know that I'm constantly afraid on runs. I just learned how to get past it, but a little fear is good. It keeps you alive a lot longer than being overconfident."

Cam's hand circles the dark bruise near the center of my chest. Ass-breath did a number on me. I'd almost forgotten the pain until Cam's touch brings it back to life. I wince once then concentrate on not moving.

"I'm going to make him pay for this," Cam says. He props himself on his elbow and leans over me, kissing the painful reminder of my failings.

"I hope we never see him again." I run my hand through Cam's brown hair, entangling my fingers in it so I can force him to kiss me on the lips and give me respite from the pain in my chest.

"We should get ready," Cam says. His face says he doesn't want to.

"I'm always ready for you." I kiss him again with my hand still wrapped in his hair, and then guide him to my aching cock.

Cam grasps my erection and strokes it slowly. I arch my back, thrust my hips upward, and fuck his hand. Thoughts of losing him earlier tonight flood my mind. I push them away and pull him closer. My lips and tongue move across his lips, the razor stubble on his cheek, and the fleshy lobe of his ear.

"On your knees."

I nibble his ear a few seconds more before rolling away from him and pulling my knees under my chest. By rote, I raise my ass into the air. Cam leans over me. He kisses my neck, wraps his arms around me. The heat and closeness of his body gives me comfort.

I hear the top of a lube bottle *pop* open, and the cold gel sends shivers throughout my body when Cam spreads it on my hole. Slowly, he presses his middle finger into me while he kisses my neck and whispers, "I love you" into my ear. I reach back and stroke his cock. A drop of pre-come glides across my finger, and I suck it off, savoring the sweet nectar.

When Cam's index finger joins his middle finger, I gasp. It's been too long since I've had him in me. We've settled for quick hand jobs or blowjobs that gave relief but not fulfillment. I've missed this, missed him. He moves his fingers in and out of me. I will myself to open up, to let him in. I want him to have me, to fill me, to take me as only he can.

Cam pulls his fingers out, and I hear him lube his cock. I breathe in deeply and arch my back. He wraps his arm around me and lifts upward. I lean forward and place my hands on the wall.

"Cam, I love you. Fuck me. God, I need you to fuck me."

I feel the head of his cock on my hole. He rubs it against me, up and down, side to side. Slowly he presses forward but stops just before he enters me. The mattress moves when he repositions.

"Lean back."

I comply and lower myself onto him. My breath catches when the head of his cock bursts through my sphincter, and he holds me there. He flexes inside me, and I resist the urge to impale myself. We both want to savor the moment, but I know that we both want to fuck with wild abandon, too.

With a hand on my shoulder, he pushes me down. By the time I'm sitting on his lap, both of us on our knees, I'm gasping and babbling incoherently. Those nonsense words you utter when you feel so close to the one you love, the one whose soul bonds with yours. I lean my head back onto Cam's shoulder and kiss him from the side.

He moves his hips back and forth, slowly at first, but then he gains momentum. Our lips lock together, our tongues filling each other's mouths. Each time he withdraws, I grip his cock, and each time he thrusts up into me, I press myself to him.

Cam wraps his hand around my cock, but I move it away. I want to last, and I know if he touches me, I won't. I need this to go on. I need to forget that zombies are real, that humans are monsters who will kill you for a can of beans.

He increases his pace, and I give myself over to him. My body is his. He breaks our kiss and whispers "Ian" repeatedly into my ear. His voice cracks and takes on an urgency of the point of no return.

"I'm coming, baby," he gasps.

"Yes, fill me up, Camden. Come in me."

The first jet of come erupts from Cam's cock, and he bites my neck to stifle a scream that would attract zombies. His teeth bruise my flesh at the same time his cock heals the bond between us. I sit down and don't let him move. The spasms of his cock unloading itself of shot after shot of come inside me elicit a moan.

"My turn," I say. I guide his hand back to my cock.

A light blinds us a second before Darren says, "Oh, shit! I'm sorry. I thought you guys would be dressed by now."

"God damn it, Darren." I reach beside the mattress and throw the nearest thing at him. My shoe bounces off his ass on the way out of our room.

"I'm really sorry." He takes up a position outside the door, his back pressed against the wall. "The others asked me to get you for a meeting. They want to know what happened last night."

"We'll be there in a few minutes," Cam says. He leans backward until his spent cock eases from my wet hole. His palm smacks against the sweaty flesh of my ass cheek, and we share a frustrated kiss.

All too quickly, he's pulling on jeans and a shirt. He drags the denim slowly over his hard ass, looking down at me with a grin that makes me want to pin him to the wall and fuck him loudly enough to draw the attention of every zombie within miles.

"This is torture." I hit him with a pillow.

He laughs the entire time it takes to put on his own shoes. "Up and at 'em, Doctor Ian."

I look down at my persistent erection. "I'm never going to shove this in my pants."

Cam tugs on me a few times. "It'll give Darren and Mandy a show." God, I don't want him to stop.

"I still think the little shit comes in here on purpose." I pull on my own jeans and maneuver my dick around until it fits, albeit with an obscene bulge. "I'm telling you, he wants to get fucked."

Cam throws me a shirt and drops my retrieved shoes on the floor at my feet. "There are worse things than a man in his sexual prime with curly blond hair, baby blue eyes, and a strong jaw. Not that I've noticed."

I ignore his description bait. There are only three gay men in the base, and Cam doesn't want Darren to be alone. "It still feels weird to think about bringing him into our bed. Not that I do." I grin at him.

With my shoes tied, and my deflating cock readjusted, I kiss Cam on my way out of the room. He smacks me on the ass. I'm going to kill Darren.

† † †

The room we use for meetings is near the east wall of the building. The two boarded-up windows let in enough light to see and be able to go about the day's tasks without having to burn candles or kerosene. Since both are in short supply, we conserve them as much as we can.

Everyone is waiting for us, with the exception of Sandy—Mandy's twin—and Ken who are on sentry duty. While Cam is the de facto leader of the group, Bert, who's straddling a metal chair, takes the position of power at the head of the white plastic folding table.

Mandy has her head down, catching a quick nap following her turn on watch the night before. She obviously wants to know what's going on before she crashes for the day. Darren sits next to her. He keeps casting glances at me, and out of the corner of my eye, I see him notice my crotch. When I stare openly at him, he clears his throat and sinks into the chair.

Bert catches the look between us, shakes his head, and spits on the floor. I ignore him. Elaine, the oldest of our group at seventy, gives me a wink when I sit next to her. She pats my leg and hands me a small can of pork and beans. I immediately hand it to Cam.

"Thanks anyway," I say to Elaine.

"The food choices don't get any better," she says.

"Especially since you two came back empty handed," Bert says. His voice, so deep and menacing, used to intimidate me. Now I realize that's just his way of trying to assert authority. "You two stop to fuck and forget what you were out there for?"

"Good morning, Bert," Cam says. "We're doing great after we managed to survive two zombies and an ambush by other survivors. Thanks for asking."

108

"Ambushed?" Mandy asks. She's alert now.

"What happened?" Darren asks. Unlike Bert, his concern is genuine.

"We got the supplies and were heading back when two guys jumped us," I say. "They told us if we tried to follow them that they'd kill us."

"Then we should leave them alone," Darren says.

Bert makes a noise that sounds like a duck getting its neck wrung. "Like that'll put an end to it, huh? How the fuck have you survived this long, dumbass? They ain't going to leave us alone."

"No, they're not," Cam says. "One of them followed us, and I killed him in front of the bakery. We need to find out everything we can about them and make a plan. Either they'll attack us, or we'll have to attack them."

"We're going to fuck their shit up," Bert says, slapping his hand on the table. "I'll go find the fuckers."

"Just don't do anything st—" Elaine cuts herself off and smiles a grandmotherly smile at the obviously pissed off behemoth sitting next to her. She pats his hand twice before he jerks it away. "That is, be careful out there."

Everyone hears Bert mutter, "Old bitch," but nobody says anything. Elaine's grin could put the Cheshire Cat to shame.

"Okay, so Bert's going to scout. Take Ken with you," Cam says. "Elaine, would you take Ken's spot at front sentry? Ian and I need some more rest, and Mandy is about five more minutes from becoming a living zombie." He pats her shoulder and motions for her to go on to bed.

"Stay safe," I say because I know it'll piss Bert off.

He scowls, makes his duck noise again, and barrels out of the room. Elaine follows him after a pat on my shoulder. Darren suddenly realizes he's alone with Cam and me. He stands up and starts to say something, but I cut him off.

"Darren, let's take a walk. I want you to help me check the supplies in the kitchen." I stand up and give Cam a kiss. "I'll be damned if I'm eating beans for breakfast again."

"Picky, picky," Cam says before spooning beans into his mouth.

"No more kisses for you." I look at Darren, and we leave Cam to his disgusting meal.

† † †

"What did you find?" Darren and I have been in the kitchen area for about five minutes, and things aren't looking good. My stomach growls at the thought of food, but since everything I see is beans, I'm not too keen on giving respite to the monster inside me.

"There's nothing over here," Darren says.

"This has to be some kind of goddam cliché," I say. "It's the zombie apocalypse and there's nothing to eat but fucking beans. I bet those assholes took some really good stuff from us last night." I sink onto a chair and stare at the seven cans of pork and beans on the shelf.

"We'll find something else."

I look at Darren, and that's when I realize he's staying as far from me as he can. "What's wrong with you?"

"Nothing." He puts his hands in his pockets and tries to have that "aw shucks, mister" look that probably worked better when he was ten years younger. His eyes take in the floor as if he's trying to memorize it for a competition.

"Bullshit."

"I'm fine. Nothing's wrong." He flashes the biggest, fakest smile I've seen in a while. "I'm going to go see if Elaine needs some help."

I stand up and plant myself in his path. It's probably a total dick move—and I'm honestly not trying to be a dick—but I want to see if Cam is right about Darren. The best approach is the direct approach. It's not what Darren wants, but it'll save the most time.

"So, which one of us do you want to fuck?" I try to keep my voice as neutral as possible. If I sound like a jealous asshole, he'll bolt, and we'll be right back at the games in a few days.

His head snaps up so quickly I can almost hear the sound barrier break. Denial paints his face before his lips start moving, but he apparently sees that I don't believe it. He sinks into the chair I vacated.

"It wasn't supposed to happen like this?"

"What?"

"Every goddam thing." He holds his arms out to the side to indicate the world at large. "As far as I'm concerned, there are exactly three fags left in the world, and I'm the one unlucky enough not to be paired up. This shit sucks. I could die at any minute, and my only way of relieving the stress of that death sentence is jerking off to the sounds of you and Cam fucking."

The look of horror on his face when he realizes what he just said is enough to make me laugh for several seconds. I know I shouldn't, but what the fuck. He accepts that I'm not laughing at him and smiles that boyish little grin.

"You still haven't answered my question. Which one of us do you want to fuck?" I ask.

"I don't want to break you two up. That's not my intention at all. I promise."

I sigh and lean forward until our eyes lock and our noses are mere inches away from each other. "Which. One. Of. Us. Do. You. Want. To. Fuck?"

"Both of you," he whispers.

I ruffle his hair. "That wasn't so hard, was it?"

"So, you're not mad at me for...for telling the truth?"

"Just like for you, the world isn't what any of us thought it would be." I lean back against the wall. "Our lives are fucked up. The status is anything but quo, and society is the piles of refuse we walk past every time we leave here. It's possible we'll find another person who's gay,

Darren, but I know you don't want to take that chance. The truth is Cam and I don't want you to be alone, either. We care about you."

"Really?"

"If we didn't, I wouldn't be here right now." I hold my hand out, and when he grabs it, I pull him into a hug. "This is probably going to feel weird for a while, but we're willing to give it a try if you are."

He squeezes me tightly, and with my luck, he's short enough that his face presses into my bruised chest. I inhale sharply, and he backs away while I rub the offended spot.

"Sorry."

I wave away his concern. "It's okay. That fucker last night got me pretty good."

"Let me see."

Knowing where this is going, I pull my shirt over my head as slowly as I can. Darren's watching me the entire time, licking his lips. I stand with my arms at my side, and I resist the urge to prompt him to make a move. His eyes rove over my body, from my furry pecs to my stomach that's getting leaner than I want.

Like a timid fawn emerging from a thicket, Darren approaches me. Using the tips of his fingers, he traces the blotch on my chest. I shiver and feel my cock stirring from his electrifying touch. It's crazy how just the slightest touch from Cam or Darren can drive me to erection almost immediately.

I want to touch him, but this needs to go as quickly or as slowly as he wants. Scaring him off isn't going to solve anything. He leaves off the bruise and runs his fingers through my chest hair. His hands travel up to my shoulders and then down my arms.

He leans close, eyes closed, and kisses me gently, tenderly on the lips. Once. Twice. I lean into it, pressing our lips together. My hands move to his waist, holding him close without force. My crotch rubs against his stomach, giving him no doubt that I'm thoroughly enjoying his attention.

Darren's lips break from mine. He kisses my chin, my throat, and drags his tongue along my jaw line and down to the hollow spot where my shoulder meets my neck. I kiss the top of his head. The smell of strawberries hits my nose, and I realize he must have found some shampoo. I'll have to ask him later. Right now...

Oh, god!

He bites at my right nipple, pulling on it with his teeth. His deliberate—or maybe it's undeliberate, who knows? Who cares?—slowness is driving me crazy. My cock is so hard it's pressing painfully into my jeans. I want to free it, but at the same time, I want Darren to—

Fuck it.

With one hand, I undo the button on my jeans and free myself. My other hand is on Darren's head, and I push him to his knees. I feed my cock to him. He opens up, and with little help from me, he's swallowed it completely. I hear muffled coughs when his nose touches my body.

I look down into his eyes. He's staring at me the entire time he slides along my cock, dragging his tongue in circles up and over it. He stops at the head, teasing the slit at the same time he sucks on me. I intertwine my fingers behind his head and fuck his face. Long strokes. Short, fast strokes.

"You're such a good cock sucker," I say.

He moans and forces all of me into his throat again. Swallowing repeatedly, he massages my cock. He cups my balls with his hand, squeezing gently, coaxing me to come.

I pick up the pace, using him for my pleasure. The look on his face—the fact he won't quit staring up at me—lets me know he's relishing every minute of this. The desire to fuck him is overwhelming. I want to see what his eyes look like when I bury myself in his ass and paint his guts white. I want to hear him scream my name and beg me give him more, to fuck him faster, harder, again.

The thought drives me over the edge. With a groan that would put a zombie to shame, I fill Darren's mouth. He swallows, and then the

113

next shot fires. He backs away, and I grab my cock. Jerking myself, I spray his face, cheeks, and lips. It drips from his chin onto his shirt.

When I finish, I rub the head of my dick through the sticky mess, slowly feeding it to him a dollop at a time. He greedily licks me clean. When the last of my seed is a drying sheen on his pretty face, I pull him to his feet and kiss him. I taste myself on his lips, his tongue. He rubs my quickly softening cock, sending shivers through me as I hit that sensitive feeling all too quickly.

"Thank you," he says, giving me another kiss.

"Go clean up," I say. "You sleep with me and Cam tonight." I slap his ass with both hands and grab two hands full. "We're tearing this up."

"I'm more than fine with that."

† † †

Cam is asleep when I get to our room. The empty beans can is sitting on the rickety table on his side of the mattress. Just looking at it makes my stomach grumble, and it reminds me we have to find food. I think briefly about Bert and Ken, wondering if they're okay, but Darren's blowjob has me thinking more about sleep.

Cam should be happy I followed through on his recommendation. We'll talk about it later. Once I've slept more than a few minutes.

My clothes stay on, and I snuggle up behind Cam. I enjoy the feel of him pressed against my chest. The slow rise and fall of his resting body lulls me into sleep like ocean waves gently tossing a boat.

I don't know if I dream. Generally, now, I don't remember my dreams unless they're nightmares of zombies eating me. Those wake me up in a tangle of sheets, screams, and dripping sweat. I hate those. Thankfully, they aren't as prevalent as they were when all of this shit started last year.

I have no idea how long I've been asleep when Elaine starts shaking my leg and calling my name. Cam is gone when I open my eyes. I sit up and look at her, and I notice all color has drained from her face. I don't ask what's wrong. Someone needs me.

We track the screams to the infirmary. Sometimes they're long, drawn out howls of agony. Sometimes muffled cries caused by someone's hand over the sufferer's mouth.

I hit the room at a run. Bert and Cam are trying to hold Ken down on the bed. Blood is everywhere, on everyone. Ken is thrashing around, howling, screaming, waving...

Jesus! Both of his arms are nearly gone—one at the shoulder, the other just above the elbow. Blood alternates between spraying weakly and splattering against walls and flesh. Bert clamps his hand over Ken's mouth to stop the noise just as I get to the table. Ken is wild-eyed and whiter than Elaine is.

"Zombies?" I know the answer because the wounds are jagged and torn, not clean.

"Yes," Bert says. His answer is matter-of-fact and cold, just like him. Cam's holding it together because he has to, but Bert... Bert might as well be looking at a bug pinned to a piece of Styrofoam.

"There's nothing I can do." I barely get those words out. It's the first time I've had to say them in a long time, and they make me want to puke.

Ken has stopped screaming, barely moves. He's going to bleed out, and I can't stop it. If Cam hadn't moved a chair behind me, I would fall onto the floor. I'm staring at Ken in the last moments of his life, with Bert's hand still over his mouth.

"What the fuck!" I scream when Bert plunges his knife into Ken's skull. I'm back on my feet while he struggles for a few seconds to extract the blade. Some of Ken's brains join his blood on the table.

"Zombie bite leads to zombies. He was dead either way. Better to be quick," Bert says. He wipes his knife on Ken's shirt and starts to walk away.

"We'll meet you in a few minutes to talk about what you learned," Cam says. He restrains me from whatever he's afraid I might do.

"Yeah," Bert says on his way out of the room.

"He just..."

"Ian, you know it was the right thing to do," Cam asks. He hugs me from the side and rests his head next to mine.

I stare at Ken's body. "We have to take him somewhere."

"We can do that tonight. Do you want to go with me?" he asks.

"Yes." No. I don't want to do anything other than curl up into a ball with Cam wrapped around me. "We can look for food while we're out, too."

"Sounds good. Let's go talk to Bert."

I look at Ken one more time before I leave the room. Our numbers are dwindling.

† † †

Bert and Ken found the other group. They're small—only four people—but they're sitting on enough weapons to hold off any outsiders. After he tells us where to find them—an old pawn shop about two miles away—he goes back out. He's going to see if he can catch one or two of them in the open.

After full dark, I wait with Darren near the back door while Cam scouts the site where we're taking Ken's body. Darren leans into me. He hasn't said more than two or three words since we started waiting for Cam to come back. He just sits there, close by, letting me know I can rely on him.

It comforts me more than I want to admit. Cam knows there's a change that has happened, but I haven't had a chance to tell him yet. Things that are more important needed my time and attention. I'll tell him before we leave.

"Here he comes," Sandy says. She opens the door, and Cam rushes inside.

"I've found a spot. It's far enough away that the body shouldn't be connected to us, but not so far that we wear ourselves out getting there," Cam says. "You ready to go?"

"Yeah." I take one of Cam's hands and put it in Darren's, and then I take his and Darren's free hands. Cam looks at Darren and then me. A smile slowly spreads across his face.

"Welcome to the family," he says. He kisses Darren, and then kisses me. "We need to go. We'll talk when we get back," he says to Darren.

I kiss Darren quickly, and then Cam and I grab Ken's body—that I've wrapped in a sheet—and we move out once Sandy gives us the all clear signal.

It's a cloudless night, and the moon is a sliver in the sky. We don't have much light, but as usual, Cam takes the lead. I try not to think about Ken too much. It won't bring him back, and it won't change anything. It just is.

"At the end of this block," Cam says. He whispers over his shoulder but his words still sound like a shotgun blast in the dead silence of the night.

Within minutes, we've placed Ken's body near the burned-out heap of a car. I take the sheet off to make it look even more like a random person caught out in the open, alone.

After a few minutes of respectful silence, I tell Cam, "Let's go try to find food before my stomach ties itself into a knot."

Since we're already in the vicinity, we head to a small neighborhood a block over from where we left Ken. Cam's been here a couple times, and he hasn't seen much activity in the area. It's a gated community, but not one of the swanky ones for rich people. This is for low-income people, who want the sense of security that a fence and gate provide. It's all just an illusion, before and now.

Cam is up and over the fence within seconds. When I get to the top, a sound catches my ear, and I stop. I can't be sure, but it sounded like gunfire. Just one shot somewhere in the distance. I wait to see if more will follow, but all I hear is a newly blowing breeze rattling leaves in.

"What's wrong?" Cam asks when I drop down to the ground.

"I thought I heard a gunshot, but it wasn't too close."

"Small favors," Cam says. He leads the way toward the nearest house.

The front door opens with a squeal that makes me jump. We stand on the porch, not moving, barely breathing, while we wait to see if we've drawn anything's attention. I count down the seconds and time my breathing with the count to keep it under control.

"This one's not too big," Cam says. "Kitchen's in the back. You focus on food. I'll check the other rooms. I'll meet you when I'm finished."

I wait for him to go in first. A quick look around lets me know we don't have unwanted guests. Inside, I turn on my flashlight and head for the kitchen. No one has picked over the house. Everything is how the family left it before crazy descended on the world.

There's a pile of toys near a wall, and a heap of clothes on the couch waits for someone who will never fold them. On the small metal table in what passes for the dining room, a ring of dried milk flakes off the sides of a pink plastic bowl. A raggedy baby doll missing an eye and most of its hair hangs halfway over the edge, contemplating ending it all on the dusty linoleum below.

The kitchen is a megabucks jackpot of food. Boxes of cereal, canned goods—other than beans, thank god!—cookies, and potato chips. My stomach growls appreciatively, and I pat it, promising it a treat as soon as we get home.

I remove my backpack, take out the extra bags we packed, and fill them. By the time Cam comes in, I've nearly finished, but the cabinets still hold food. It's a happy predicament.

"You find anything useful?" I ask.

Cam holds up a .45 and a small case of bullets. "This is the best thing, but I also found some toothpaste, soap, and mouthwash in the bathroom. Oh, and some more toilet paper, thankfully. "

"Can you fit any more food into your bags?" I ask.

"Some, but we shouldn't take everything all at once," Cam says. "We don't want to be weighed down if we get into a bad situation. Besides, I doubt it's going anywhere since it's been here this long."

We get a few cans of soup and a jug of water that I spot near the back of the pantry. We're good to go, and I kill the flashlight, giving both of us a chance to get our night vision back. Cam leads the way, stopping near the door to listen outside. When he gives the signal, we step out onto the porch.

Well, shit!

"You know, boys, we keep meeting like this, someone might start talking." Ass-breath laughs and slaps his friend—who is pointing a rifle at us—on the back. "See, Rog, I told you the pansies would do the work for us."

"Fuck you." I expect the words to come from Cam, and then I realize I said them. Of course I did. I suppress a groan and wait for the fallout.

Cam is standing just in front and to the right of me. We slowly place our bags on the porch, moving slowly so "Rog" doesn't get the wrong idea. When we stand up, I can see Cam's hand moving slowly to the .45 he tucked into the back of his pants. I make a small noise and step closer. I'm not as good a shot as he is, but Ass-breath and Rog shouldn't be able to see me going for the gun.

"What did you say, faggot?" Ass-breath asks.

I've obviously pissed him off, but I can't do anything about that except stay alive. Besides, it's the apocalypse, and it seems we've run into this inbred redneck fuck-head more than we have zombies. What is up with that?

Ass-breath swaggers toward us, and I step closer to Cam. Rog apparently doesn't like that because he tells me, "Don't fucking move!"

I stop because I'm close enough, and I pull the pistol out of Cam's pants.

"I asked you what you said, faggot." Ass-breath is halfway between his friend and us. He places his hand behind his ear and cocks his head to the side. "I'm waiting, boy. You had a mouth on you before, which isn't surprising for a cocksucker. Cat got your tongue all of a sudden?"

"Something like that," I say.

Cam dives to the side, and I bring the .45 up. Ass-breath is still oblivious, but he starts moving when his friend shouts. It's too late. I've squeezed off two rounds. Both of them hit—one to the shoulder, one to the arm—and Ass-breath goes down, screaming like a little girl. Who's the fucking pansy now, bitch?

I realize Rog should have fired and taken me out by now, but he hasn't. Instead, he's standing there shaking and...crying? What the hell?

"Drop it, Rog, or I swear I'll drop you." It's a terrible line, but it has the desired effect. He throws the rifle on the ground and puts his hands into the air.

Cam jumps off the porch and runs to the still-screaming Ass-breath. He pulls a pistol out of his holster and puts it to the guy's head while covering his mouth. Blessed silence.

I leave the porch and walk out to Rog. He's definitely crying, and I don't know whether to feel pity or disgust for him. The sound of breaking glass in two different directions down the street drowns out whispered apologies.

"Company," Cam says.

I put the gun to Rog's nuts while I bend down to retrieve the rifle. "This thing loaded?"

"No," he sobs.

"What kind of dumbass walks around with an unloaded rifle?" I ask.

"He doesn't trust me with bullets because I don't like killing people," Rog says.

"Talk later. It's time to move our asses," Cam says.

"You should run," I say. "Go back to your friends."

"I won't make it. Please take me with you."

Shit.

"Go grab the bags off the porch. You try to run, and I'll shoot you in the fucking leg and leave you. Understood?" He's gone before I stop talking.

A distinct moan emanates from the trees across the street, and I hear brush and bushes rustling. Ass-breath stumbles past me, and I look at Cam over my shoulder.

"He's going to be trouble," I say.

"Right now he's an insurance plan. If he acts up, he's bait," Cam says.

"Fine with me."

"Let's go," I say when Rog runs up with the bags. He's looking around nervously.

"I won't make it over that fence," Ass-breath says.

"How did you get in here? And what's your name?" I demand.

"Scott."

"Of course it is. Lead the way, Scotty, and no fuck ups," I say.

The zombies pick up their pace. There are five of them, and I'm sure the gunshots and screaming have drawn more toward us. Cam follows Scott at a run toward the fence. I motion for Rog to follow, and I'm close on his heels.

A zombie lunges at me from the right. I had no idea it was there, but I have enough time to put a bullet into its head. Making more noise isn't going to do anything but add to our problems, but I have to risk it. We have to get back.

Scott leads us through a gap between two trees. I fully expect him to try to take advantage of the situation and either run or attack Cam, but he proves smarter than that. We all make it through, and take off running as fast as we can. Zombies come from multiple directions, getting closer the farther we go.

"We aren't going to make it," Rog says repeatedly.

I tell him to shut the fuck up and focus on running. He keeps wasting breath on muttering the mantra, but at least I don't have to hear it as much. Scott and Cam slalom around piles of debris and abandoned cars.

When I finally spot the outline of our base a block away, I look over my shoulder. My heart sinks. We've gathered a following that trails back as far as I can see, which granted isn't that far in the darkness, but still I know they're there.

"Cam, take Scott and the bags. Rog and I are going to lead them past and try to lose them," I say.

"Fuck no," Rog says.

"Shut up." Cam stops long enough to grab a bag, throw it at Scott, and then take the last one. He kisses me and then pushes Scott toward the back door.

"Run." I turn and shoot two zombies near the front of the pack and catch up to Rog. "We're going to the store where you and Scott jumped us last night. We'll go in and sneak out the back. I still have enough bullets to shoot you, so don't try anything."

"I won't. I promise," Rog says. "I was just with those guys so I wouldn't get killed. I'm not like them."

"Sure you're not."

† † †

It's almost dawn before we make it back to base. Rog is dragging. Well, I'm dragging him. After we succeeded in getting away from the horde, Rog gave out when the adrenaline stopped. I asked myself several times why I was risking myself for someone who had robbed me and would have probably shot me if he had ammo.

The likely answer is because I want to believe we can reclaim society, and we can't do that if we turn into monsters too. Part of it is also my pledge to do no harm. I've had to break that far too many times since this all started. Scott's proof of that, even if his circumstances don't exactly fit the spirit of the oath.

Rog collapses seconds before Mandy opens the door and looks from me to him. I shrug, and she helps me pick him up. She bars the door behind us, and I drag Rog to the infirmary.

A few feet from the room, I smell burnt flesh. It gags me, and rouses Rog long enough for him to throw up. He's cleaning that shit up later. Not my job. In the infirmary, I dump him on the floor and look up right before I bump into Bert.

He's got a knife held under Scott's chin. Scott looks at me with a pleading look that I take far too much pleasure in ignoring.

"He giving you trouble?" I ask Bert.

"Naw. We cauterized the wounds since we didn't know if you'd be back. Besides, we can't have a prisoner bleeding to death. Pretty sure that violates some convention or another." Bert laughs and the movement causes Scott to gasp. A drop of red runs down his neck and absorbs into his shirt collar.

"Easy does it. Don't kill him until we get a chance to find out about his friends and their base."

"Oh, don't worry about them. They've been dealt with," Bert says.

"Dead?"

"One of them. Other one is in worse shape than your boy here is. He might not make it. Not my problem," Bert says.

"Did you take the bullets out first?" I check the wounds that Bert probably took great joy in heat-sealing.

"Nope."

"Well, he'll probably live. Not sure if that's a good thing or not. You have this under control, Bert? I need some sleep."

"I'm good. Scott and I have us a little understanding. He doesn't piss me off, and I don't lobotomize him, right?"

"Yeah," Scott says, licking his lips.

"I doubt this one'll give you any trouble, but I can find something to tie him up if you want," I say about Rog.

"I'll get to that. These two are cake."

I don't know if that's a jibe at my expense, but I'm too tired to care. My bed is calling my name, and I don't intend to keep it waiting.

† † †

Darren has wasted no time moving into the room Cam and I use. He's brought his mattress and the few belongings he's scrounged up the past few months. Cam is big spoon, and when he apparently senses me standing at the end of the mattress just watching him, he opens his eyes.

"Glad you're safe," he says with a smile.

"Me too." I sit down, and it's the greatest thing I've experienced in hours. "Sorry I woke you."

"Not really sleeping. I can't when you're not here." He pulls his arm from beneath Darren's head and shakes feeling back into it. "Did you eat?"

"Too damn tired for that," I say. "In the morning."

"Isn't it morning already?"

"Who the hell can remember?" I stand back up long enough to strip off all my clothes then lie down.

"You need to eat." Cam's tone pisses me off. Not because it's condescending or hateful, but because I'm so goddam tired.

"Later. I need sleep more than I need food." I face away from him and pull part of the pillow over my head to end the discussion. A hand resting gently in the center of my back causes me to tense at first, but then I relax into the gentle touch I hadn't realized I needed so badly right now.

I wake up later, laying on my back, my cock in Darren's mouth. Propping myself on my elbows, I watch him deep throating me while Cam fucks him slowly. Cam smiles at me.

"Hope you don't mind," he says.

I shake my head. Darren pulls off both of our cocks at the same time. Straddling me, he lines my wet dick up with his ass and takes me all the way in. He moves in slow circles while squeezing my pecs. He leans forward to kiss me and slowly fucks himself. Cam strokes his own cock for several seconds before moving behind Darren.

"Holy fuck!" Darren shouts when Cam's cock joins mine in his tight ass. He stops moving and starts panting.

I pull Darren to my chest, kissing the top of his head and whispering soothing, encouraging words to him. His insides spasm as if he's coming, but I know he's just trying to adjust to the amount of hard meat he's taking. When he latches onto one of my nipples with his teeth, I curse and tweak one of his nipples in return.

Little shit!

I wrap my hand in his curly hair and pull until he willingly lets go. My lips press against his, and I shove my tongue into his mouth at the same time I thrust my dick deeper into him. Cam and I take turns, setting up a nice rhythm of one thrusting in while the other pulls out.

Darren moans into my mouth. He's leaking pre-come all over my stomach. I massage his balls, pulling them down and gently tugging on them. From the sounds Cam's making, I know he's close. I want us to blow at the same time so I pick up my pace. Darren's tightness coupled with the unexperienced friction of my dick on Cam's pushes me closer to the edge.

When Cam screams, a hot blast of come rushes over my cock into Darren, and I lose it. My grip on the blond locks of hair in my fist tightens, and I throw my head back, screaming as loudly as Darren and Cam. We fill Darren at the same time he blows a load onto my stomach and chest.

He sits up and sprays my face. Come runs out of his stretched hole, making all of us a sticky, sweaty mess. I don't think we'll ever get clean from this.

When they both collapse on top of me, I can barely breathe, but I'm too high to complain. Cam is still hard inside Darren, and he's slowly thrusting in and out, keeping me hard. Darren whimpers, but I feel him trying to thrust back onto both of us.

By the time I catch my breath, Cam has fired off a few more shots into Darren. He slips out and collapses onto his back. Darren kisses Cam and then me. Sweat pours off him onto my chest. I'm still inside him, and he leans back, pushing me as deeply into him as he can. He sits there, moving in slow circles, relishing the fullness.

I sit up, kiss him, and wrap my arms around him. He rides me with his legs wrapped around my waist. Cam is on his knees beside us, taking turns kissing us. Darren picks up his pace, riding me, fucking himself with exuberance.

When I come, it's a cross between pain and pleasure. Cam surprises us by spraying our chests with another load. Darren's sexual energy apparently isn't just invigorating to me alone.

"You guys...are fucking amazing!" Darren leans against me, kissing my neck and shoulders. Come oozes from his cock in a steady stream, pooling between our bodies. He's finally spent.

"I don't know if I can do that every time," Cam says.

I laugh and start to say something when a loud noise causes all of us to jump and stare at the doorway. We hear someone scream, "They're inside!" and we don't bother with clothes. We all grab knives and run out of the room, down the hall. Shouts and screams get louder, coming toward us.

Elaine falls backward at the end of the hall. Two zombies are on her. She's hacking at them with the broken remains of a butcher knife, but there's no way she's going to make it long enough for us to get to her. When one of the creatures falls on her neck, sinking its teeth into her, she shrieks for a few seconds before lying motionless.

Darren and I take the zombies while Cam ensures Elaine rests in peace. We move on into the room past her body. Bert is a whirlwind of slashing knife and machete. A pile of rotted bodies is at his feet. So much blood, viscera, and extra flesh cover him that he's almost indistinguishable from the zombies.

We finish off the stragglers at the fringes before Bert says, "We've got to close the back doors." He takes off without seeing if we're coming.

When we get to the back of the base, Mandy is fighting a losing battle. Sandy is dead on the floor with a knife in her heart. Zombies struggle to get into the doorway. Those already inside press toward us; they want a meal. Bert throws his knife into the skull of a biter at Mandy's back. She drops one in front of herself, oblivious to Bert's actions.

When we join them, we hack, slash, stab, and do everything we can to stay alive. We're almost demon possessed if our shouts are any indication. Bodies choke the doorway, and slowly we work our way over the pile, forcing the fight outside.

I'm sure the battle lasts only a few minutes, even though my body is saying it goes on for hours. When Darren drops the last zombie, I lean forward and puke. I'm exhausted, covered in things I'd rather not think about, and mad as hell.

"How did they get in?" I ask.

"That little fuck, Rog," Bert says. He spits on one of the bodies. "He got away from me."

"And killed Sandy," Mandy says. She's kneeling beside her sister. Before Cam can offer to finish Sandy, Mandy pulls the knife from her twin's heart and drives it through her forehead.

"I didn't figure we needed extra shit to deal with, so I offed Scotty when I figured shit was going to get intense," Bert says without batting an eye.

"Elaine was at the doors, and it didn't take much for Rog to get past her," Mandy stands up. She won't look at any of us. "By the time I got back here, they were already coming in. I thought we were dead."

There's nothing we can do about the doors. One is barely hanging on, and a mound of death buries the other one. Anger bites at my stomach and my heart the way a zombie chews through flesh. I look at Cam, and he nods.

127

"Everybody get your shit," I say. "This place is done."

"Where are we going?" Mandy asks.

"Rog probably went back to his base. We're going to pay him a visit."

Silver Magic

By J.C. Quinn

He's calling me again. I can feel the pull in my chest, like my heart is off balance, beating toward the north. I ignore it and try to finish eating. *Thump, thump, thump.* The feeling stretches into my arteries and veins. It pulls until my entire chest cavity aches. And, like Pavlov's dog, my dick starts to twitch.

I drop a handful of bills on the table. I haven't gotten the check yet, but it doesn't matter. I left enough. Money isn't an issue, as long as I'm on Morgan's good side.

Everything takes too long. The walk to the subway station, the train, the sitting on hard plastic while my pants get more and more uncomfortable. I close my eyes and concentrate on nothing. Just the black void and bursts of color behind my eyelids. Breathe, in and out— no, wait. Don't think of in and out. That doesn't help.

My skin tingles with the throbbing. It goes all through my body now, down to the tips of my fingers, my toes, and my cock. I stumble out of the metro station, into the neon night. It isn't cold out, but I still pull my hood to protect myself from the world. Any sensation is too much right now.

I hit the buzzer outside his apartment building.

"Hello?" He says, his voice full of smoke and rum.

"Let me up, asshole."

The electronic lock *thunks* open and I head upstairs. My pants tighten and loosen with every step up, like the worst, slowest, clumsiest, most maddening hand-job in the world.

The big, gold letter C on his door came unscrewed on the top and hangs upside now. It swings a little with each of my knocks.

The lock clicks open.

I want to play it cool, I really do. But I'm throwing the door open and telling my feet to stop running down the narrow entry hall.

The whole place is dark and heavy with the smell of patchouli and dragon's blood. Old, thick rugs cover the scarred hardwood floor. Behind me and with no visible force, the door slams closed and locked again. Candlelight leads me to him, sitting on the dining room table, one foot up on the chair, and a glass of blood red wine in his hand. He tosses his hair out of his eyes, but they're still obscured by layers of black, smoky kohl. On the table behind him is a small bowl of fire, a jar full of salt, and the toothbrush I used when I was here last week.

He smiles, slow and crooked, when I come into view.

"Stop." He waves his free hand at me and hops off the table.

His pants, black leather because he has to play into every stupid cliché, hang low on his hips. His shirt is open, revealing the thick, totally not fake silver chain around his neck and his slightly muscled stomach. He turns his head and takes a long drink of wine. The way the light flashes on his throat as he swallows makes me forget to breathe again.

He sets the glass down and walks towards me. One step, one more, then the next, it's going to take him a century to get here. I'll die, right here, with an erection threatening to break through my fly, hating everything, especially his stupid, pretty face.

His hands touch my jaw sending jolts of electricity from my jaw straight to my crotch. There's a sound from somewhere, like a moan. It takes me a moment to realize it's coming from me.

"Jesus, Morgan." I put my arms around him and pull him against me. "I need to fuck you."

He chuckles, but it's little more than hot breath against my chest. "Not yet."

I groan. I hate how whiny I sound. How whiny he makes me sound. My heart still pulls the strings in my body, wanting to get closer to him. I don't think it'll be close enough. Even when I'm inside him, I want to go deeper and deeper.

His fingers spider down to the button of my pants. On his tiptoes, he kisses me, the corner of my mouth, my jaw, that soft part of my neck that beats and beats and beats for him. He makes a sound that vibrates against my skin and snaps my pants open with one hand.

"God, Ethan, please." I cup his head in my hands and kiss him hard. Pushing my tongue past his teeth, into the hot wetness of his mouth. He tastes like cloves.

And suddenly, he's gone. A rush of cold fills in the space where he was. He goes back to the table, undoing his pants as he walks, shimmying out of them. With a flourish, the wine sloshing over the sides of the glass, the chair spins around to face me. He sits and spreads his legs slightly, the grin still on his stupid face.

"Blow me, first."

Something like gravity forces me forward, between his legs and on my knees.

"I hate you," I say, resting my hands on his knees.

He leans down and licks the tip of my nose. It's playful and the one side of him I like, but I frown because fuck him.

I run my hands up the insides of his thighs and my tongue from his balls to the head of his dick. *Yes, please, fuck him.* His cock is long and thin, fitting into my mouth perfectly and bumping against the back of my throat. I fight my gag reflex, flexing around him. He shudders and runs his fingers roughly through my hair.

He slouches in the seat, giving me more room to move, but I don't want to lose him. The musky-salt taste of his precome and sweat fills my mouth as I inhale the heady herbal smoke smell that clings to his skin. I want to be closer.

Please, I try to say, but I've never been good at talking with my mouth full. The vibration sends goosebump shivers through his body. I grip his ass cheeks and pull him toward me, driving him deeper in my mouth, *but it's still not enough.* A sound like air escaping a balloon comes, unbidden, from my throat.

"Who's my good boy?" He purrs into my ear.

The head of his penis drags across my cheek as he stands up, leaving a trail of saliva and precome. Warm at first, but cooling quickly.

"Goddammit, Ethan." I get as tall as I can while still on my knees and open my mouth to catch him again, but he stops me with a whisper and a wave of his hand.

"If you're so eager, maybe you should have come when I first called."

"Well, I'm here now and I'd like to come."

He drops down to my level and kisses me. "You're not nearly as clever as you think you are."

His hands fall to the hem of my shirt and lift it over my head, stopping at my wrists. From this close up, I see the magic happen. The words are smoke-scented puffs of air on my lips. Red light sparks around his blue irises. The fabric of the shirt tightens around my wrists. I look up. The white cotton is now crimson rope, binding my hands together.

"Fortunately for the both of us," he puts one hand between my legs, massaging my balls through the denim of my jeans, "you're not here for your wit."

I gasp and take his bottom lip between my teeth. He squeezes me hard and harder until I yelp and let go.

132

"No one likes a bottom trying to top." I pout.

Another smile breaks across his face. "Liar."

He puts my bound hands around his neck, forcing me to hold him close, and guides us both to standing. Turning, he presses his naked body against mine. I forget how to breathe for a minute while he brings my arms down around his waist.

"Promise not to keep me waiting again?" He arches his back, pressing his ass into my groin.

I make a sound that loosely resembles a "yes."

"Good boy."

With one hand, he reaches back and undoes my fly. Without the aid of anything natural, not even gravity, my pants fall to the floor, boxers and all. He bends over, elbows on the mahogany table, and pulls me with him. I thrust in deeply, hugging his hips close to me, going as deep as I can.

Now he's the one moaning uncontrollably. The candles flare and wane with every thrust into his tight ring. All of the muscles in my body clench as I—

"No!" he shouts at me, the candle flames all freezing in place. "Don't you fucking dare. Not yet."

Dammit. I lean over him and kiss the back of his neck, slowing the in and out pumping. Kisses turn to nips and bites. He throws his head back. The fires flicker. The pile of salt flattens a little more every time I drive into him, shaking the table. I pull almost all of the way out before pressing back in as far as I can go.

It's an awkward position until I realize I can lay my chest against his back and reach his cock. I take it in both hands and stroke him in time to my fucking, which matches the beat of my stupid, traitorous heart that leads me here every week.

I work the silver magic out of both of us, filling him up with mine and spraying the floor with his. My shirt falls from my wrists, freeing my hands just in time to catch Ethan as he swoons. He grins at me, all dopey and drunk on the afterglow.

In the morning, I slip out of bed like a ninja. I pick every hair off the pillow case. I take that fucking toothbrush and shove it in my pocket. No trace of me at all. No sympathetic connections for him to latch onto and call me back. He doesn't even know my name. I smile, going over everything one last time to make sure it's clean. Then, I fold up my boxers and shove them under the couch cushion.

He's going to have to work for it.

The Devil Made Me Do It

By Gio Lassater

I stand beside the mangled remains of my car. Gasoline and blood assault my nose and the back of my throat. Lucifer grins and admires his handiwork. After all, he caused the wreck. A wave of dizziness sweeps over me, and I hold my head in my hands while I lean forward and throw up.

"I think I'm dying." I wipe my mouth clean. If only the sun would hurry up and set, I wouldn't be able to see the red-tinged remnants of my late lunch on the moss-covered ground.

"Well, you might want to hold off on that," Lucifer says. "If you die before you give me my consolation prize, your soul is mine."

I suddenly realize he should be a demon, but he looks human. Long brown hair is held in a ponytail close to the crown of his head. He checks his well-manicured nails and brushes something from his white suit. I'm sure there was nothing there, but I hope it was a piece of my vomit.

"I said I'll get Michael, and I will. I've already made preparations at my apartment."

Lucifer steps forward and I feel heat rolling off him. It soothes me; washes over me. I can almost pretend that I haven't made a deal with the devil. That I haven't fucked up my life—both before and after the deal—to the point that he wants me to corrupt an archangel.

"Not just corrupt," Lucifer says. "I want you to fuck him. I want you to make him give in to his carnal desires."

"Why?"

He grabs me by the throat and picks me up. I cough. Flecks of blood rain down on him, but he ignores it. Fire, real burning fire, dances in his eyes for several seconds before he puts me down. I fall onto my knees.

"Is that a sufficient answer to your question?" he asks.

I can only nod.

"Good." He grips my shoulders and stands me up. Moving close, he brushes my lips with his. White teeth draw my attention, and I stare at his rictus smile as a forked tongue licks my blood from around his mouth. Lucifer's hand massages my dick through my dirt-caked pants. I want to pull away, but the stimulation feels too good. It helps me forget I'm probably closer to death than I've ever been.

"I'm going to go now. Pray for Michael to help you. It has to specifically be him, or just anyone can show up." The pressure on my erection becomes painful. "You don't want anyone other than Michael, or else I will drag you to hell and let a demon with a barbed cock fuck you while you drown in a pool of liquid Sulphur."

He disappears, and I fall onto my knees.

"God—" I stop myself. I have to focus and get this right. "Michael." I close my eyes and press my hands together in front of my face. The smell of the vomit I'm kneeling in assaults my nose. "Michael, I need your help. I think I'm dying. Please, I know that I haven't done anything to deserve your help, but please help me. Please, you have to. I don't want to go to—I don't want to die."

On the highway at the top of the slight embankment before me a car drives past too fast to notice or care about the missing guardrail I took out when Lucifer wrecked my car. I lurch forward, intent on crawling. The ground is cold beneath me, and I long for Lucifer's warmth.

"Michael," I whisper. Dirt and blood coat my lips, and then the inside my mouth when I lick them clean. I spit. "Michael, I need you. Not going to make it."

I hear another car. There's a bright flash of light on the road, and then the car is past. I press my forehead against a small patch of moss. Another flash catches my attention, especially since there isn't a sound associated with it. Rolling onto my back, I stare up at the sky and realize the sun has set.

"Is—" The attempt to talk sets off a bout of coughing that echoes into the darkness. When I stop and can breathe again, I make another attempt. "Is someone there? Michael, is that you? Help me!"

"You need assistance," a man says. A soft light surrounds him, and I know that it's an angel. Lucifer didn't tell me what Michael looks like, so I can't assume that's who he is. Either way, his beauty stops my breath and causes my heart to beat faster. Brown hair cascades down onto the shoulders of his brilliant white robe, and cobalt eyes stare into the soul that I've sold to the devil.

I wonder, briefly, if he knows what I've done before I say, "Yes, I do. I desperately do. Are you Michael?"

He bends down and picks me up in his arms. Warmth radiates from him the same way it did from Lucifer, but this doesn't conjure horrific images in my mind. I wrap my arms around him and lay my head against his chest. I'm surprised when I hear his heartbeat, but I stop thinking about it when the rhythmic sound fills my ears.

He speaks words I cannot understand. The world around us goes silent. I've never felt power before, but I can tell this is it. The real deal. Miraculous and ancient, it's meant for my benefit. I close my eyes and push away my guilt. It's him or me. The thought of Lucifer's promised punishment pushes me forward.

As life seeps back into me through Michael's prayer, I brush my lips along the soft, iridescent flesh of his neck. He falters over a word but forges ahead. His words become louder. I kiss his neck. I bite on his earlobe and whisper my thanks into his ear. He lowers me until I'm standing in front of him, and I press my body to his.

His voice returns to a softer tone as his prayer nears an end. I feel my flesh made whole again. The taste of dirt and blood leaves my mouth. Aches and pains disappear. I'm alive, completely alive. Well, for the moment anyway.

"Thank you." I kiss his lips, but he doesn't reciprocate.

"You are well now?"

"Yes. Are you Michael?" I try to keep the sound of desperation out of my voice, and I'm mostly successful.

"Yes. Why did you pray for me specifically?" he asks. "I'm not usually tasked with these sorts of things."

"Yours was the name that came to me when I realized I was probably going to die." The lie sounds natural to me. I hope it does to him, too.

"I will take you home, and then I must leave. There is much I must do."

He takes my hand in his. I shield my eyes from the blinding white light surrounding us, and when I can see again, we're standing in the cramped confines of my apartment. Michael looks at the bare tan walls, the pyramid of beer cans, and the shattered remains of too many whiskey bottles.

His natural luminescence flickers, and he frowns. Closing his eyes, he whispers a few of the strange words again, and his glow returns to full force. It only lasts a few seconds, though, and then he steps backwards.

"I have expended more energy than I thought. May I sit down?"

None of the chairs are accessible due to cans and bottles, so I lead him into the bedroom and point at the bed.

"Do you need some water?" I ask.

He nods. When I return from the kitchen with his drink, Michael is staring at his hands. He accepts the glass and downs the contents. Without asking, I get him more. The second time he goes more slowly. I watch him and gently massage his shoulder. His warmth is not as pronounced as it was at the wreck.

That thought drags my attention to the small stand beside my bed. I will myself to move slowly toward it and the dusty scroll Lucifer gave me. The words I recited are no longer visible, but I don't want to take chances. The power-dampening spell is proving effective, but if Michael knows what's going on, there's nothing to keep him from just walking out the front door.

I toss the scroll into the stand's drawer and then crawl across the bed. Kneeling behind Michael I massage both of his shoulders. He groans before grabbing my hands and putting a stop to my actions.

"What are you doing?" The question is a demand for immediate response. Even with the spell, I can feel his power.

"Relax. You've spent a lot energy on me, remember?" He removes his hands from mine, and I go back to kneading his flesh through his robe. "Thank you, by the way. I don't think I've said that."

"It is what I do." He moves his head in a slow circle and then finishes the last bit of the water. "That feels very nice. Thank you."

"You're welcome." I have no idea how to proceed from here. Lucifer didn't really give me any tips on how to seduce an angel, and it's not as if I've had much luck with humans. "Do you want more water?"

He contemplates the glass and says, "Yes."

I refill it and again watch him drink all of it. When he finishes, the glass explodes, sending shards in all directions. I scream and clutch my stomach. Risking a look down, I move my hands and see blood pouring from multiple holes. Michael's eyes are wide, and he shakes his head.

"That should not have happened." He touches me, and I suck in air, trying not to scream again. He speaks more words, but nothing happens. He repeats the words, but still there is nothing. "There is something wrong. I am unable to heal you."

"It's okay. It's not that bad."

"Then why did you scream?"

"I was...surprised by what happened." I move his hand away and pull off my shirt. Tiny holes litter my stomach. Blood trickles over my abs and into the waist of my pants. "I've got some first aid supplies in the bathroom. Why don't you come help me?"

I take both of his hands in mine and pull him to his feet. He's a few inches taller than I am, and I stare up into his eyes, mesmerized by him. Without intending to this time, I stand on my tiptoes and kiss him. He stands stoically for several seconds, but then I feel the slightest return of pressure on my lips from his.

We move into the bathroom adjoining the bedroom. Towels litter the floor, and the small trashcan should have been emptied weeks ago. The small sink and counter are bare except for dust, hair, and dried gobs of blue toothpaste. I lead Michael past all of it to the shower in the corner. The glass door screeches open on its rusted hinges.

I turn the knob, and the water blasts out in a scalding-hot torrent. The thought of just jumping into it crosses my mind, but I twist the knob back a quarter turn. I unbutton my pants and let them fall onto the floor.

When I get into the shower, I turn and look at Michael. His eyes are practically glued to mine. He won't lower his gaze, but we both know that he wants to. Lucifer was right; this should prove to be easy if I don't blow it.

"Get in. Help me." I reach my hand out to him. "Please."

Michael closes his eyes. His sigh is audible over the sound of the shower. Just when I think he's going to turn around and walk out, he grabs his robe near his waist and lifts up. Beneath, he's completely nude. He doesn't even wear shoes. The robe joins my stuff on the floor. He stands still.

I wiggle my fingers at him. "Come on." I fake a wince and grab my stomach. I don't have to fake too much, especially once I make contact with my abdomen. It hurts like hell. The vision of being fucked by a demon with a barbed dick flashes through my head. Okay, maybe not exactly like hell.

Turning into the spray, I let the water pelt my face. It runs down my body. I stare in sick fascination at the pink water swirling down the drain. I squeeze some body wash into my hand and rub it onto my chest. Almost immediately, my wounds start burning. My knees start to buckle, and the world begins to tilt slowly to the right.

Michael's hands grasp my shoulders, and he keeps me upright. I lean back against him. His chest is so solid. His muscles feel so amazing against my back.

"I don't know why, but I can't heal you." His words are filled with regret.

I pull a piece of glass out of my stomach and hold it up where he can see it. "There are seven more of those. One's pretty big. I'm going to need you to get them out."

I turn around and look down at his dick, wrap my hand around it. Michael licks his lips and brushes his hand over my chest. My focus stays on getting him erect, but it wavers when he starts with the big piece of glass.

I stifle a scream.

"I'm sorry." He kisses my forehead. "I wish I could heal you. I don't know why my power isn't working."

"You've said that. Don't worry about it." I take a deep breath. "That should have been the worst one. Get the others out and then…" I lean forward and kiss him. His cock is so hard in my hand.

Michael presses his tongue into my mouth. He makes quick work of the rest of the glass. Once, I bite his tongue, and he stops until I release the pressure. As soon as the last piece is gone, I fall on my knees and suck his cock into my mouth.

He utters more nonsense words. His grip on my head is strong and urgent. If I hadn't been so eager to suck his dick, he would be fucking my face with it. As it is, I have to resist some of his insistence. The head of his cock grazes the back of my throat. I hold it there for a moment. My tongue swirls up and over the shaft. Then I swallow him.

The glass enclosing the shower explodes. I should be dead, cut to ribbons, but it all disappears. I see it dissolve when I look up. Michael's head is thrown back, but then he looks down at me. His face is nothing but bliss. We make eye contact, and he smiles. I didn't think I'd ever see that.

I back off and stand up. "Have you ever had sex?"

"Your wounds are healed."

"What?" I look down. He's right. There's no trace of anything on my stomach. Things are going to be tricky if sexual pleasure gives Michael the ability to circumvent the dampening spell.

"Have you ever had sex?" I have to keep him distracted and focused on the pleasure, not on what he wants.

"I... No." He licks his lips. "We should not be doing this."

I stroke his dick. It's still as hard as it can be. "Something tells me there's part of you that doesn't agree with that. I'm not going to force the issue, but if you want to fuck me—and I mean *fuck* me—then let's do this."

I turn off the water and leave him in the shower. Thankfully, there's a clean-ish brown towel hanging on the rack, so I wrap it around myself and go back into the bedroom. With the towel around my waist, I crawl across the bed and lie in the center of it, propped up by pillows.

"Take that off," Michael says when he enters the room. He's still erect, and I can tell by the set of his shoulders that he's made his decision.

I look down at the brown terry cloth then back at him. "Are you sure?"

"Yes."

He watches me as I pull the towel off and toss it across the room onto a pile of shirts in the corner. His dick twitches, and a drop of precome drips onto the carpet at his feet.

"You have an amazing body and such a big cock," I say.

"Thank you." He moves to the bed after I've settled myself again. Bracing himself with his hands on the edge of the mattress, he leans down and kisses me. Our lips brush against each other. I let him be in control because it's hotter, and it keeps him focused on something other than leaving.

Another drop of precome forms, and I swipe it off with my thumb. It's sweet on my tongue. I share the taste with Michael. Our tongues entwine in his mouth. He may have never done anything like this, but he definitely knows what he's doing.

Michael presses his crotch against my hand. His glides over my stomach, and for the first time he touches my cock. Unless I knew better, I could swear that his power goes all through me. His touch is electric. I immediately harden in his hand. He tugs on the shaft, hesitantly at first, but then he gives in to the desire I know he has. From the base to the tip, he strokes my cock.

I lean over and begin sucking him again. From the corner of my eye, I watch his hand making love to my dick. He's so tender. Just when I feel the urge to tell him to stop being so gentle, he bends down and swallows the entirety of my erection. His nose presses against my balls. The urge to come, to explode in his mouth, is overwhelming. I clench the comforter, close my eyes, and back off his dick so I can focus on my breathing.

Michael groans, and the added sensation drives me closer to the edge.

"Stop, please, or else I'll come."

He sits up and looks at me. "But I thought that was the point of this."

"It is. Eventually." I laugh. "First, there's longing and pleasure. There's driving your partner to the brink of release, and then letting them down from that so you can take them there again. There's also my desire to have you inside me. You've got to fuck me, Michael. I need you to fuck me."

"Why? Why do you need this?"

"It's just an expression." I move to sit on my knees in front of him. "I want your first time to be special. I want you to enjoy it. For me, that enjoyment will be having you inside me."

I smile, and I wish he would too. He doesn't, so I pull him into an embrace and kiss him. Our hands move over each other's flesh. I grab his ass and circle my finger around his tight hole. He mimics my actions, but he goes a step further and presses his finger until it almost goes inside. My hips gyrate, and he moves with me. Always on the precipice. Never beyond.

Slowly I kiss down his neck. Lick my way across his pecs. Bite his nipples. My tongue swirls across his abs. The entire time he bends farther and farther so he can continue to finger me. By the time I'm back at his cock, he has two digits inside me.

Michael's cock drips precome almost steadily. I lick him clean and suck him. I move slowly. By the time I press my nose against the flesh of his waist, Michael is crying out, begging me to stop. He threatens to lose control and fill my throat with his seed. Even though his fingers are still inside me, they haven't moved for several minutes. I move all the way off, and then I swallow his cock all at once.

Michael grunts. I glance up at him. Blue fire erupts from his eyes, and his dick spasms. I grip his balls, squeezing them, rolling them in my palm. I pull back, and jet after jet of come coats my tongue.

The room echoes with his gasps and moans as I milk him dry. I release him, and he collapses onto his side on the bed. Sweat covers him from head to toe. He gasps for breath.

"You're still hard," I say as I lay beside him.

"I haven't been inside you yet," he says.

I smile. "No, you haven't. Now would be a good time for that." I kiss him.

He rolls me onto my stomach and moves between my legs. Gripping my ass in both of his strong hands, he spreads me open and buries his tongue into my cleft. I lift my ass into the air, and he takes advantage of my eagerness, darting his tongue against the quivering ring of muscle.

I rock back and forth, fucking myself with his tongue. Reaching back, I press his face deeper and hold him there. His tongue moves across my hole, opening me for the inevitable onslaught of angelic cock. I moan into the comforter and beg him to fuck me.

His fingers replace his tongue, and I thrust my ass higher into the air. I hear him spit. Looking back I watch him smear the saliva onto the head of his dick. He's so hard that I'm certain he could come several more times and never go soft. I don't know that I can ever sate the desire I see in his eyes.

His cock rests against my willing hole, and then he eases into me. Grasping my hips, he pulls me back while preventing me from impaling myself on him. He wants to enjoy it. I want him to enjoy it, but not as much as I want him to fuck me. I beg him to fill me. He promises he will.

Fully enveloped in the inviting confines of my ass, he presses himself to me. Michael wraps his arms around my chest. He bites my ear and rocks his hips. I turn to kiss him over my shoulder, and his cock slides in and out of me. First, it's a few inches, but quickly it becomes the entire length. From the tip to the balls, he gives it and then takes it away. The sensation drives me crazy.

"I'm close," he says.

"Wait." I make him stop. "Lay down on the bed."

He looks confused, but he complies. I straddle him. He's soon inside me again, and I ride him. With my legs on either side of him, I bounce up and down. Alternating between long and short movements, I pleasure both of us. When I can't take anymore, I bottom out on him.

My orgasm erupts from me with a scream. Long, thick ropes of come stretch across Michael's torso. One shot hits his lips, and he licks them clean. He locks his gaze with mine, and then I feel him coming inside me.

"Yes, come for me, angel. Come inside me. Oh, yes!"

He lifts me up slightly and then thrusts repeatedly, coming the entire time. I lean forward to kiss him and milk the last drops from my spent erection. All too soon Michael slips out of me.

I collapse onto his chest.

"You were amazing," I say.

"Thank you. I have never felt anything like that." He kisses me. "I am sorry, but I must go now."

I roll off him. He moves to sit on the side of the bed. Now's the time. I have to do it. I have to. I close my eyes and run words over in my head. It took me almost a full day to memorize them, and if I don't say them now, I'll never say them.

I just don't want to.

Michael walks into the bathroom, and when he returns he holds his robe in his hands. My come runs in rivulets down his chest, stomach, and legs. I want him to just come back to bed and fuck me again, but that's not going to happen.

"I'm sorry, Michael. I have no choice."

The words—ancient words that I don't know or understand—move from my memory to my tongue and take life in the stillness of my bedroom.

"What have you done?" Michael tilts his head to the side and furrows his brow. His body goes rigid before a flaming sword appears in his hand.

"What I had to." The lie is ashes in my mouth.

The lightbulb flickers and then dies with a *pop*. A cacophonous din of screams and agonized wailing assaults me. I press my hands against my ears to block them out. The walls move inward and outward like the room is gasping for breath.

A phantom hand draws a ring of fire on the floor, and a black-skinned demon with broken wings materializes inside it. He thrusts his hand toward Michael, and the sword is extinguished. Michael falls onto the floor, clutching his throat.

"Hello, dear brother. Time for a visit." The demon's voice sounds like murder.

Michael struggles as an unseen force drags him into the demon's hands. Before he disappears, he looks at me, but I turn my head in shame.

"You've done well," the demon says. "Lucifer said your debt is now paid in full."

They disappear in a column of orange-red fire that scorches the ceiling.

Raising the Stakes
By Gio Lassater

God, I hate Paris. It figured I would finally track Aramaeus here. I looked at my surroundings—a cheap, trashy knockoff of the infamous Moulin Rouge. I had heard so many things about Aramaeus, but the fact he frequented this establishment in this city made me judge him more harshly.

Why couldn't it have been Istanbul? Or even Rome? Either of those would have been more fitting for the task ahead of us. But, no, he had to flee before I could spring my trap, and so, we were left with Paris.

A courtesan with enough makeup on to outfit an entire circus troupe dragged her hand along my arm in what I'm sure she meant to be a seductive manner. Looking up, I shook my head slightly and realized why she slathered on foundation with a paintbrush. Not only had life been cruel to her, but someone had obviously decided her looks weren't hideous enough. Many men had beaten her. She attempted to persist, but I cast the look at her I usually reserved for the worst of my prey, and she quickly got the picture.

Through a large window I saw a bolt of lightning flash across the sky. The raucous music drowned out the peal of thunder that followed, but the rumble added to the earthquake-like trembling of the dance hall. Raindrops pelted the dingy window panes. I feared the weather would dissuade Aramaeus from presenting himself.

A waitress, her bosom barely contained by lace and prayers, moved close to the divan I had laid claim to, and I asked her for a pint. She shook her head and leaned in closer, asking me in French what I had said.

Having spoken in Italian, I asked again in the language she understood. She nodded, I slipped a few francs into her cleavage, and she disappeared into the scrum of drunks, dancers, and dandies. Within moments she returned with my glass, and I sat nursing it.

As the clock struck midnight several pints later, the main door opened, and a man in a hooded black cloak stepped inside, brushing away heavy droplets that bespoke the last fury of a storm outstaying its welcome. I held my breath.

The cloak swung out and away from the man in a well-practiced and unnecessary flourish. I finally had him.

Glancing at the tall, burly bouncer to the left of the door, I nodded. He winked at me in return and stepped forward to assist Aramaeus with his things, escorting him toward the bar. Soon, libation in hand, the bouncer led Aramaeus to my location and indicated he should sit.

I pretended nonchalance and disinterest at first. I did not want to put Aramaeus on guard. Having never met me before, he would not suspect I was who I was. No need to send him running again.

"So much flesh, the eyes do not know where to look first." He had leaned toward me to nearly shout the words into my ear.

With a sideways glance I responded, "But there are some things better left to the imagination."

"Oh, do you have an imagination, friend?" He quirked an eyebrow at me. I could tell he thought he was being subtle, but the way he closed the few inches of space between us told me I intrigued him.

"There are many things I can imagine, and even more I can enjoy." I rested my arm on the wooden frame running along the top of the divan's back. It projected an image of budding intimacy I knew he would see as a victory.

His right hand sat atop his knee; the delicate lace cuffs at his wrists looked like a cloud, light and soft. I felt his small finger brush against my leg through the fabric of my trousers.

"I, too, have an excellent imagination." He leaned closer to me, his lips mere centimeters from my ear, and whispered, "What I can't imagine is why the council would send a human to hunt me down—even a human as stunningly handsome as you are."

"Xander warned me that you are a keen observer." I placed my hand slowly atop his, letting him feel the steady beat of my heart. He should know I was not afraid at having been discovered so easily.

"How is dear Xander?" he asked. "I haven't seen him in ages. Still attempting to live out his aspirations of being king?"

"He is the high prince now," I said.

Aramaeus's eyes briefly widened, but he regained his composure quickly. "Is that why you are here? Am I to be brought before him in chains? Is that it, human?"

"No," I said. "That is not his intent. I have been sent to you to indulge you. Xander wished for you to have a taste of something you have never had before."

"I've had many things," he said. "What makes you think you can give me anything new?"

I mimicked his actions from earlier, leaning in toward his ear. However, I did not stop until my tongue had traced along the lobe and half way up the pinna. I felt him shiver beside me. "I was trained by Damian."

He moaned softly. "You *are* a prize." He glanced around the room, and I could feel the various eyes that were taking us in. "We should leave this place. My kind is seldom welcome, and the fact that you just did what you did is ruffling some feathers."

I tightened my grip on his hand. "Know this, Aramaeus, if you run again, you sign your own death warrant. My orders are clear. If I have not bestowed my gift on you by morning, you will be exiled from court for all eternity."

"Well, Xander certainly knows how to give *gifts*, doesn't he? Very well," he said, "You shall bestow your gift upon me, and then our exalted prince can live out the rest of his life knowing duty was done by one and all. Shall we?"

At the door, the bouncer handed me my coat and hat, which I donned quickly. Aramaeus left out the flourish while pulling on his own cloak.

He offered his elbow to me.

Against my better judgment I slipped my arm through his, and we stepped into the damp aftereffects of the late spring thunderstorm.

"Your place or mine?"

I moved in the direction of my rented chalet. "This way. All my arrangements have been made. I believe you'll be quite pleased."

"Oh, I have no doubts." He chuckled and pulled me closer to him. "So, Xander specifically chose you, did he? Why? What makes you so special?"

"You wouldn't want me to give away all my secrets, would you?"

"Honestly? I haven't decided." He inhaled sharply. "Although, I will say the scent of you intoxicates me. Do you have control over that?"

"As a disciple of Damian, yes. I've expended a great deal of my powers on you. The fact that you have eluded me for so long just means that tonight will be even more..." I leaned closer to his him and whispered, "satisfying."

He shivered and laughed. "Well, then I must say that I'm not sorry I ran from you all these months. I cannot begin to imagine what tonight holds for me."

"I thought you had a great imagination."

† † †

The large wooden door opened at our approach to the chalet.

Aramaeus stood in the center of the main entryway, turning in small circles as he took in the opulence of the marble, busts, and priceless works of art that adorned walls befitting a palace.

"So, where shall our grand adventure climax?" he asked.

"This way." I led him through a short hallway to the left, taking him through the dark kitchens and down a rustic, creaking staircase at the far side of the house.

"There is no telling how long we might last. We don't want the sun to put a premature halt to our revelries." I pushed open a heavy wooden door bound with iron straps and indicated he should precede me.

Once inside, I closed the door, and turned at the sharp hiss emanating from Aramaeus's lips. "This is no trap. If you wish to leave, you have but to say so, and you are free." I moved away from the door, indicating the golden crucifixes attached to it. "You leave only if you ask it, or if I grant permission. Otherwise, you are to stay here until the ritual is complete."

He attempted to not look at the objects causing him pain. His fingers gently grasped the drawstring of my blouse, and I stepped toward him when he tugged me. Our lips met in a soft kiss I would never have thought him capable of.

"I will endure… for you, and for the promise of an imagination broadened." He walked away, looking around the room. "So, where, how do we begin?"

"I prefer to take my time. Is that your choice as well?"

He cocked his head to the side, resting silky black curls on the pale white fabric of his own blouse. "I am amenable to whatever my host decides. It is my ritual, but it is your task. Why shouldn't we both enjoy it?"

"Slow it is, then," I said. "You may sit while I prepare, if you like."

He bowed deeply to me before sitting on a high-backed wooden chair with a purple cushion, his right leg draped over the arm in an attempt to display his crotch for me.

I had previously lit two candelabra, but I wanted more light. To behold Aramaeus in all his resplendent glory I would need to light every candle in the room, so I did. It took several minutes to complete, but the reward was worth the effort.

When I looked back at the man I had sought for so long, I felt my pulse quicken. His cold, gray eyes followed my every movement while a finger absentmindedly twirled an ebony lock of hair. He had loosened the draws of his blouse, exposing the smooth pectorals beneath. I imagined running my hands over them, feeling the hardness.

He closed his eyes, rubbing his left hand over his crotch. "You must hinder your smell, or else I will not be able to contain myself," he warned.

I took a deep breath to be able to sense what he had. My power suffused the room. With great effort, I brought it under control. No other man had ever elicited this response.

"Is that better?" I asked.

"Yes, thank you."

With the candles lit and my power under better control, I moved to the chains hanging from the ceiling near a corner of the room, testing them to ensure they would not easily dislodge.

Satisfied with their integrity, I lit several sticks of incense. The room filled with a smoky haze that heightened my senses to the same level as my guest.

"Shall we begin?" I asked.

Aramaeus smiled and stood up. "I thought you would never ask."

I held up a hand to stop him in my tracks. "There are forms to be observed if you wish to continue."

He sighed. "I'm listening."

As I spoke, I walked toward him. "I am in control. You do what I say, and only that. If you refuse, the ritual ends. You will be chained. If you break even a single link, the ritual ends. If you harm me in any way—"

"I get it," he said. His eagerness was getting the best of him.

I should have been flattered, I guess, but instead it made me angry.

"No." I let the word hang between us, drawing out a silence that I knew tortured him. Finally, I said, "If you harm me in any way, all your progeny will be put to death. If you kill me, you will be tortured for eternity."

"Xander does not play games, does he?"

"He does not. Neither should you. Do you wish to continue?" I asked.

By then I had stopped in front of him, clearly inside the zone most men would find uncomfortable. While he gave off no warmth, seven centuries of accumulated power flowed through him and brushed along my senses.

"I wish to continue," he said.

I felt myself begin to fall into his eyes. "You may not glamor me. That is considered an attack."

"So what *can* I do?" he demanded, his voice bordering on petulance.

"You can enjoy the ritual," I said.

With great care, I undid the laces of his blouse, pushing it over his shoulders. He moved his hands behind his back and allowed the garment to fall to the floor. The alabaster beauty of his flesh seemed to reflect all the light from the candles.

Hesitantly I reached out and rested the palms of my hands above his chest, not making contact but still close enough I could infuse him with minor tendrils of my power.

He inhaled sharply; his head fell back, and an ecstatic moan escaped his lips. "That is amazing," he whispered. "What do I call you?"

I pulled my hands away. "I cannot tell you my given name. To do so would be to break the spell that gives me my power. What would you like to call me?"

He contemplated me for a moment, licking his lips. "Your green eyes remind me of my first love—Paul."

"I would be honored to be called by his name," I said.

"I want to kiss you, Paul." He stepped forward. "Please, may I kiss you?"

I pressed my chest to his, wrapped my arms around him, and drew him to me. Our lips met as softly as they had with our first kiss, but when I unleashed my power into him, I thought Aramaeus would devour me. I felt the sharpness of his teeth and had a momentary vision of them sinking into my neck. More power flowed from me, and suddenly he was on his knees.

"Stop. Stop, please. You overwhelm me." He panted. "By god, what are you?"

"A mortal who sees something he wants," I said. "Enough games. This begins now. Stand."

He did as I instructed, but only with my assistance. Once certain he would not fall over, I dropped to my knees before him and undid the fastenings of his breeches. I took great care not to touch his flesh, and all my power withdrew from him. He would remain flaccid until I wanted to experience the hardness that yearned to break through the fabric. With a single thought I forbade his flesh to follow any impulse but mine.

"Sit in the chair." He obeyed my commands, and I removed his boots and socks. Slowly—achingly slowly—I pulled his trousers down, exposing the smallclothes he wore beneath them. I left those in place in order to tease myself and delay my own gratification.

I urged him to his feet, drawing him away from the chair, and had him stand with his legs slightly apart while I walked slow circles around him. His muscles, which would not have changed once he underwent the Great Transformation, bespoke a hearty and robust mortal youth that surely had men and women alike throwing themselves at his feet.

"Who were you before you became Aramaeus?" I trailed a finger along the muscles of his back. In front of him again, I gently rubbed his right nipple while flicking my tongue over the left.

"I was a prince, first in line to the throne," he said with a hint of sadness. "My father loved me with all his heart and gave me everything I ever wanted. It broke him when I changed." He cleared his throat. "My name does not matter. I am Aramaeus, now and forever more."

"Forgive me for dragging up sadness when you should be experiencing bliss," I said.

He caressed my face. "There is nothing to forgive. Please, continue."

I grasped his hand and led him to the corner with the chains I had tested earlier. "Brace yourself. This may hurt," I warned. I locked one manacle in place.

He hissed, his gray eyes clouding over. "These are silver."

"Yes," I said. "Do you wish to stop?"

"Do not ask me that again," he commanded. "I have started, and I *will* finish." He reached over and clamped the other cuff around his own wrist.

"Very well. Wait here."

He chuckled. "I have no choice, unless I wish to break the chains, which I don't." He stepped out of his smallclothes when I pulled them to the floor. His cock, like the rest of him, was a work of art.

Leaving him naked in the corner, I moved behind a partition a few feet away and removed my own clothing. When I revealed myself to him again, I wore nothing but black leather boots that reached almost to my knees.

He gasped. "You have betrayed me!"

I looked down at my chest. My vision momentarily locked onto my quickly hardening erection, but I tightened the power in my groin, becoming flaccid once more. Under control again, I looked at the blood-red mark on my chest—a crow clenching a rose in one foot.

"So, you recognize the mark of the Gideonites," I said.

He spat in my direction, but the glob landed on the floor instead of on me. "Butchers and assassins! Is that what you are, Paul? Did you bring me her for a ritual, or am I to die?"

"That remains to be seen. Xander has not made up his mind. He has left your fate to me." I retrieved a dagger from a small stand and slowly drew it across my left index finger. Dangerously close to Aramaeus again, I showed him the blood.

When he leaned forward to lick the scarlet trickle, I dropped the dagger and slapped him across the face as hard as I could. He roared, his fangs elongating, and he jerked the silver chains. Dust and wood splinters rained down on both of us.

"You partake only if I allow it. I am in control." I wiped the blood on his lips to tempt him. He left it where it was. "Very good."

"Fuck you."

"Oh, believe me, you will," I promised.

"I will split you in half with my cock and feast upon your entrails," he screamed.

I punched him in the face. "No harm, remember? Not unless you want to pay the ultimate price."

"If it means killing one of your order, I would gladly pay it." He jerked on the chains again.

"I do not know your fate. That depends on you," I said. "However, you are to be punished for killing Xander's ward."

He barked a laugh. "You mean that little bitch Neisha? I did him a favor. She plotted to murder him."

"Where is your proof?"

"I have none. You know this, or else we wouldn't be going through this charade," he said.

"Then I will be your judge, and if you do not persuade me, you will not leave this room alive." I kissed him before he could speak, tasting my own blood on his lips. My tongue pushed it into his mouth, and I felt a surge of strength within him.

Our cocks rubbed together, and my power, which was keeping both of us flaccid, wavered. I reinforced it, and he groaned, pressing himself to me. A surge of my pheromones sent a shiver through him. The hunger in his eyes rivaled that in his groin.

"I am going to fuck you like no one ever has," he promised.

"Good."

I kissed his neck, trailing my lips down to his nipples. I kissed them before running my tongue over them and pinching them. My journey continued, circling my tongue around his navel, before I fell to my knees to worship the cock straining against my power.

I locked eyes with him and slowly flicked my tongue over the glans. Reaching behind him, I pulled his ass cheeks apart and ran a finger around his most intimate opening. I put just enough pressure to almost breach his sphincter, but I didn't enter him.

I took him into my mouth, stretching his cock to the point I was sure it was painful for him. Still, I refused to allow him to get hard.

I repeated this until his knees shook. "More," he begged. "I need more." He thrust his hips forward, obviously hoping to ram his soft cock into my mouth, but I pulled away.

"I am in charge. I give or take what I want. You submit to me and my power." I bit his cock to prove my point, tasting blood.

He screamed, but I could tell there was ecstasy mixed with the agony. "God, yes!"

I spit out flesh and blood, watching as his abilities took over, and the wound on his abused member healed. "So, you like pain? That opens many avenues."

I withdrew a silver crucifix from my boot. His instincts forced him to draw away from it, but the rough wooden walls behind him hindered his escape. With painstaking slowness, I held the holy object to his right nipple, moving it in a circle.

He screamed, pressing himself into the wall while his cock strained to become erect. "Release your hold!"

"No." I moved the crucifix for his left nipple.

His screams intensified; his mouth a cavern of agony. I filled it with a vial of holy water he had not seen me pick up as well. Smoke rose from his tongue and gums, and he spit red water into the air. It landed on his face, chest, arms, and genitals, eliciting more screams.

"You must be purified," I said.

"Fuck you!" Aramaeus panted. He thrashed in a futile attempt to fling the water from his body. Tendrils of smoke wafted upward. My power kept the drops in place, pushed them beneath the surface of his flesh.

Within moments his knees buckled, and the silver manacles cut into his wrists. Drops of blood cascaded into my hair, and I took his cock back into my mouth. I pressed the vial of holy water into his rectum, spilling the last of its contents.

"Why did you kill Neisha?" I asked. His screams drowned out my question, and I asked again.

"I told you. She plotted to kill Xander."

"Why didn't you tell him?" I licked along the length of his dick, burrowing beneath it to bathe his balls with my tongue. I loosened my power's grip on his cock and felt it twitch against my forehead.

"He wouldn't have listened," Aramaeus whispered. "He loved her. She would have killed him before he was willing to see the truth."

I took one of his testicles into my mouth, suckling it, bathing it with spit. My tongue dragged along the strip of flesh leading to his ass.

"How did you kill her?"

"Please, I'm telling you the truth," he said.

I constricted the power, crushing his cock. When his screams died down, I repeated the question.

"I glamored her and had her jump from a bridge."

"That is impossible." I glanced up at him. "Her mind would have rejected that order."

He stared into my eyes and unleashed his power on me. In that briefest of moments that stretched from my birth to my death while impaled on his raging cock, I learned the true scope of Aramaeus's power. He could kill with glamor—something no other vampire could do.

He released me, and I fell on my ass. My hand wrapped around the dagger I had dropped, and I drove it into his leg. The expected screams did not come.

"I was only proving a point," he said. "I would not have hurt you. Nothing would be served by it."

"What was served by Neisha's death?" I withdrew the dagger and tossed it aside.

"Xander lives," he said.

"So the ends justify the means?" I asked.

"Not always, but in this case I would say they did." He looked at the still-smoldering patches on his body. "I've grown used to this pain."

"Very well." With my power I pushed the holy water deeper into his body, completely through his arms. His screams renewed. "We're nearing the end."

"Of the pain, or of my life?"

"That is yet to be determined." I relaxed, allowing water and blood to flow from the wounds. He struggled to keep his legs straight.

I nuzzled my cheek to his, releasing more pheromones and tightening my power at his crotch. My lips smothered his, and even in his weakened state, he returned the kiss with passion. His fangs grazed along my tongue in a display of self-control I knew would be impossible for a lesser being. He wanted my blood. He needed it, but he denied himself the taste as much as I denied both of us the satisfaction.

I presented my neck to him. "You may drink. Slowly."

Hunger flashed across his eyes. I leaned in, watched his lips part, his fangs extend. Violence and blood-lust hung between us. My power boiled beneath my skin, ready and willing to repel or kill him if he gave in to baser instincts.

Aramaeus surprised me with his gentleness. His fangs pierced my neck. His lips sealed over the wound, and he drank slowly and with great purpose. I infused him with my power, giving him extra life and energy he would not have received from my blood alone.

He gasped, and I felt blood trickle down my neck, and mingle with the thick wiry black hair on my chest. I pressed against Aramaeus when he resealed my wound with his lips.

"That is enough."

He immediately released me. His wounds healed, but my blood smeared in spots on his chest. Slowly, I massaged it into his milky skin, losing myself in the eyes that wanted to wrest control of mind from me.

"Are you better?" I asked.

"Yes. I could get used to feeding on you," he said. He pushed against my power. His mind brushed mine, giving me fleeting glances of him drinking from me at the same time he thrust into me over and over.

I stumbled back a step. "Stop. That is a violation of the rules."

"I say it's time that rules be damned," he growled. "I've seen your mind. You want me. My games have only caused your lust and desire to heighten over the past few months. You barely contain yourself enough to not have raped me as soon as I set foot inside the dance hall tonight. Call me a liar."

I reached up and unlocked the manacles, freeing his hands. He shook his arms to return feeling, and I snatched one, kissing at the silver-induced wounds at the wrist until they had healed completely beneath my lips.

"You are no liar." I embraced him, reveling in the thrill of touch and power intermingled when he returned the gesture. "I feel the sun will rise soon. We must complete the ritual."

"You still have not decided?" he asked. "Even after all I have endured and shown you."

"You have not shown me your true self," I said. "But you will. Come."

I led him to the opposite end of the room and pushed him down on a rough mattress filled with straw. Sitting atop him, I rubbed my ass on his straining cock, still keeping him flaccid.

"This grows tiring. How can we fuck if you keep me contained?" The frustration in his voice matched what I felt myself.

"Patience. Allow me to do my job."

He sighed and nodded.

"Relax. Open yourself to me," I commanded. "If it is to be, then it will be. If not, then you will die beneath me."

He said nothing, only closed his eyes. I felt his barriers dropping as I probed along them. Licking the dark patches left by my blood on his chest, I moved up to kiss him gently. My tongue ran over his fangs, tasting iron on them still.

I ground my ass on his cock, flexing my glutes so that he slid in and out of my crack. I had another vision of him inside me, filling me, drinking me. Taking advantage of this, I pushed back into his mind, searching for the thoughts that would vindicate or condemn him.

A mental door slammed in front of me. Still not ready.

I kneeled between his legs and forced them toward his chest. A line of spit dripped from my mouth onto his quivering hole. Aramaeus wrapped his arms around his legs, and I leaned in, running my tongue along the ring of muscle, working the spit into him.

"Oh, god," he whispered. "Yes, Paul, yes."

I felt a hand on the back of my head, pressing me forward, and I obliged his desires. My tongue darted out, pushing against his natural resistance. With a small amount of power, I pushed beyond the ring, giving him the sensation of being fucked at the same time my tongue lubricated him. I relaxed my hold on his cock, allowing blood to slowly rush into it, knowing the frustration would heighten his senses and dull his ability to force me from his mind.

As my tongue probed his ass, my mind probed his. I saw a flash of Neisha. A finger joined my tongue, opening him wider. I heard a woman's laughter echo through Aramaeus's mind. Two fingers widened the sphincter. His muscle clamped onto my digits when I felt him enter Neisha's mind.

"Relax. Give me what I need," I told him.

"I need release," he begged.

"It will come. And so will you. But first I get what I want. Relax, and give it to me, Aramaeus. Complete the ritual."

Another string of spit worked into his hole, and I added a third finger. His resistance grew instead of waning. I knew what I must do. With little thought, I released the power that I exerted on my cock, allowing it to immediately engorge. Without warning, I pressed the entire length into Aramaeus.

He screamed. His abused ass clenched and unclenched around my erection, driving me insane. It took every bit of my training to hold back the rush of my seed. I wanted, needed release after the titillation and torture I had forced on myself.

I gave him no time to adjust to me. Rocking back and forth like a pendulum gone wild, I hammered his ass. From tip to balls, I filled him over and over, breaking down the barriers in his mind.

"Give in. Let me in."

"You're in," he grunted. "Oh my god, are you in!"

"Your mind. I have your body; now give me your mind." I continued my momentum.

Slowly, the flashes became longer, more intense. Neisha resting in Aramaeus's arms. His mind entering hers. She was strong. He was stronger. She resisted. He persisted. Her barriers fell. He entered her mind, and she was his.

I heard her screams.

Then I saw the plans unfolding before me. Neisha conspiring with a member of the Council to assassinate Xander. I saw the silver-tipped stake he—yes, it was a man—handed to her. She would go to Xander. They would make love. She would murder him while he took his rest.

I buried myself into Aramaeus, holding myself deep in the recesses of his welcoming, quivering hole. He screamed and cursed, begging me to fuck him more. Fuck him harder.

And then I saw Neisha's conspirator. I had what I needed. Aramaeus had told the truth.

I exploded inside him. I forced my power into him. Still I denied him an erection, although I let him experience every bit of pleasure he wanted and had given to me.

I had never experienced an orgasm such as this!

I collapsed onto Aramaeus's chest, my still-engorged cock buried in him, spasming. Sweat poured from me, raining in large, salty drops onto his tight flesh. Slowly I withdrew from his body. He moaned the entire time, fighting to keep me inside him.

"Stay in. Please. I know you have the power."

I pushed all the way back in while smothering his mouth with mine. He wrapped his legs around my waist, slowly gyrating and moving my cock in circles inside him.

"You feel amazing inside me," he whispered when our lips parted.

"The ritual still has not ended. You must take your turn. Only then can judgment be passed."

"There is time. I want to experience more or you before I take my retribution." He moaned when I hit a certain spot inside him. "I intend to repay you double what you have given me," he promised.

In the blink of an eye, he had me on my back. Sitting atop me, still impaled by my cock, he pinned my shoulders to the floor and slowly fucked himself with me. I felt strength and power from him unlike any other time since we began.

"The rules still apply," I warned. My heart hammered in my chest. He had frightened me with his sudden reversal of positions. I hated it, but I had to admit it to myself.

"No harm will come to you," he said. He leaned down, staring into my eyes, and I felt the glamor caress my mind. "However, I am going to fuck you the way I want to fuck you. I am in control now. You are mine. I will do with you as I please, and you can do nothing to stop it."

"You *will* stop this now." I attempted to sit up, but when that proved useless, I unleashed a wedge of power directly into his chest.

He didn't budge; he laughed. The glamor pushed deeper and deeper into my mind until I could feel him rummaging around in the deepest corners of my mind.

"I know your name."

"Don't say it."

"I won't." He kissed me, and the glamor receded, but not before he used it to access the core of my power. "That belongs to me now."

I gasped when he turned it against me, forcing me to come inside him again with only a thought. He bucked up and down, fucking himself more and harder. I struggled to regain control, but he held me at bay.

Finally, I collapsed from near exhaustion, and only then did he stand up. My come trailed from his ass. Even though I had filled him, I suddenly felt a great emptiness.

"Don't worry, I will fill it," he said in response to my thoughts. Our minds were linked.

He grasped his semi-erect member and shook it up and down as he towered over me. "Your mouth needs to be on this."

Without thought, I was on my knees. I drew him into my mouth, bathing the cream-white flesh with my tongue and spit. I could feel him slowly releasing my power's hold over his erection. It grew steadily, hitting the back of my throat. He drew back as it grew more and longer.

"Look at me."

I looked up and in defiance of his control over me I grabbed his ass and forced him deeper into my throat. He attempted to pull back, but the pleasure he felt lessened his hold on me, and I drew on decades' worth of training at the hands of Damian himself to reassert my dominance.

I am in control, I thought at him. *My ritual. My rules.*

"Paul," he whispered. He gave in, and I sucked, licked, and slurped on his unleashed cock like a starving man given food. His fingers clenched in my hair, forcing himself deeper into my willing throat. He screamed in pleasure, urging me onward.

I felt come rising within him, but I forced it back down with my power. He whimpered, begging me in my mind to allow him release. I denied it to him and pushed the blowjob as long as I could—until his cries for mercy became ecstatic sobs.

I spat out his cock, watching my saliva drip from the head and pool between my knees. "You are well-lubed. Now, you are going to fuck me like you've never fucked anyone else in your life."

He nodded numbly, waiting for my next command. I stood and turned, leaning forward until I grasped the ankles of my leather boots. My waiting hole was inches from his cock, which bobbed up and down. I gave in to the glamor, allowing Aramaeus to think he was gaining control again.

He stepped forward, grasping his dick at the base. The glans hit the resistance of my hole. I relaxed, welcoming him, inviting the invasion of a most sacred place in my body, which only one other had ever had the pleasure to worship.

I moved toward him as he moved toward me. His hands separated my cheeks, his fingers digging into my flesh. He wanted to thrust forward, to fill me with all of himself, but I forced him to resist. I forced him to move at a painstaking slowness that pleased both of us.

First the head, and I made him stop. It had been so long. Aramaeus deserved to be inside me, and I wanted it. I needed him to fuck me as if my very life depended on it. That wasn't necessary for the ritual, but it would be a fitting end for such a magnificent man who could and had fucked everyone he ever desired.

More and more I allowed him to penetrate me until I felt the smooth, unblemished flesh above his cock meet my sweat-slicked ass. He stayed balls-deep inside me for several minutes, both of us enjoying the rush of power and intimacy.

Blood surged to my head, made me dizzy, and Aramaeus took advantage of my momentary lapse. His hands became iron, and as he gripped me, he pulled all the way out and rammed his cock back inside me—once, twice, a third time.

I tightened my grip on my ankles and fought to remain conscious as he plowed into me over and over, our balls slapping together. When I felt I could take no more, I grabbed a hold of his ass and brought him to a halt. My breath was ragged. Sweat cascaded into my eyes and dripped from the stringy strands of my hair.

Aramaeus slowed his pace, moving side to side to come at my hole from different angles, rubbing against my prostate. A shudder went through both of us.

"I can't maintain this position," I said.

He pulled out, and grabbed me by the neck when I stood up, forcing me onto my knees on the straw-filled mattress. From behind, he held my head down, mounted me again, and began pounding my ass anew.

His thoughts invaded mine through the glamor, and I allowed it. I wanted him to have all of me—body and mind. If I could have given him my soul, I would have, gladly.

"You must come inside me," I said.

"You didn't need to tell me that."

I felt come rising in him again and withdrew my magical hold. Let nature take its course. Let him fill me to overflowing. He was in my mind, then, laughing.

"I am near." His warning followed an increase in his pace and shortened thrusts. Our flesh slammed together, filled the air with the glorious sounds of animalistic sex and the scent of delicious debauchery run rampant.

Aramaeus screamed in my mind and then aloud. Jet after jet of hot come flooded into my guts. My power went crazy. It enveloped both of us, and I could see a blue glimmering hue surrounding us. I blasted the mattress with several streams. Reaching back, I massaged his battered balls, milking the rest of his life-giving seed into me. He fell forward, crushing me beneath him, and buried his fangs into my neck. He drank deeply, coming the entire time.

By the time he finished drinking and filling me, my power reached its pinnacle. Aramaeus screamed, flung off my back but suddenly unable to withdraw from me. I immediately shut him out of my mind, and retrieved a wooden stake from beneath the mattress. Swinging around and back with all my strength, I slammed the point into his chest.

A blinding light and a deafening roar, and then splinters of wood exploded in all directions, burning instantly into ash before they did any damage.

Aramaeus looked down at his chest, and I knew from his thoughts he expected to be dead.

"What does this mean?" he asked. He looked at his chest then back at me. His cock still quivered inside me, refusing to deflate even though he had filled me.

"It means you are innocent," I said. Sighing, I collapsed onto the mattress, pulling him down on top of me. We kissed over my shoulder. "It also means we are bonded."

He stared at me, confused. "Bonded?"

Yes, I thought. *You are mine, and I am yours. We are linked, irrevocably.*

He smiled, wiggling around so his cock buried deeper inside me. "There are worse things I can imagine."

"The sun is up," I said.

"I know. I felt it rise an hour ago."

"You should rest," I said.

He kissed my ear. "There is plenty of time for that. Later."

About the Authors:

To learn more about the authors go to www.inkubuspublishingllc.com.

You can follow Inkubus Publishing LLC

Twitter: twitter.com/InkubusPublish (@InkubusPublish)

Facebook: www.facebook.com/InkubusPublishing

Cover Design by:

TatteredWolf Studios is the joint venture of husband and wife team Brad and Megan Baker (otherwise known as Loni and Tatiyana Wolf). The goal of TWS is to bring their unique design aesthetic to the world through traditional, digital, and video game art.

They can be found at www.TatteredWolfStudios.com.